TABLE OF CONTENTS

TAKE ANOTHER STEP

One step, quite possibly, begins the gradual adaptation that changes the whole trajectory of our lives. Muster, the bravery to breach the familiar, break the knowns, and blast beyond the realm of convenience into the tense workspace of the refinery. Being made whole, mature, or ready is praise worthy. However, being made new is another setting to celebrate. Yet, the process of being made new is arduous. The brevity of our lives elevates and escalates the importance of intentionality in what we do without a second guess every single time. Otherwise, we become experts at finding a reason not to, and avoiding the labor-intensive critical inquiries and syntheses that chart new paths and engages the discovery of better processes. Procrastination is the assumption that the option will always be available. It is more difficult to regret than to rebuild and rebound. We do well to recall that the past has nothing new to say to us, yet we are often fighting the lure to have a deep, elongated conversation with it. Sights beyond a current position prevent tomorrow from looking exactly like yesterday.

Ultimately what matters is that you focus forward by making the most of your "now". If it is true that moving forward is moving on. Then, not moving at all is counter productive, altogether.

It's not too far-fetched to compute that being out of place is because we have not allowed God to order our steps

The prospect of some difficulties pressing forward into the Promised Land, causes us, at points, to shirk back into the certain death in Egypt. This should not be the case. Change requires that I change too, and many times, FIRST. The persons who will scrutinize your improvisations are the same people who don't stick to the script themselves. So, do not allow what they think to hold you up, hold you down, hold you back, or hold you hostage. We all are walking through life at different paces. Sooner or later we catch our breath or get our second wind.

Prayer:

Lord Almighty, God of every living thing. I know that you know my every weakness. I ask you to strengthen, stabilize, and show me the way forward. I cannot make it without Your presence and power in my life. In fact, I cant even walk without You Holding my hand. Guide me forward, attract me to people who can serve as ushers in destiny's trek. I want to be a living portrayal of the Gospel, unbound. Thru your empowerment, I have victory over trepidation, intimidation, discrimination, and procrastination. I am courageous because You created me to be brave. I am unstoppable because You made me, unmade, and remade me, perpetually. Point me forward and keep me in Your Will, O God, AMEN.

Application:

Explore Where have I been holding back What have I allowed to Stop me? WHY?

_____

—

_____

—

_____

_____

—

AFFIRMATION:

BRAVELY GOING FORWARD I AM ONE STEP CLOSER to ARRIVING TO NEW BORDERS and OCCUPYING BETTER SPACES.

THERE'S MORE TO GIVE

Scripture:

Each one must give as he has decided in his heart, not reluctantly or under compulsion, for God loves a cheerful giver.

- 2 Corinthians 9:7 ESV

"The problem with hoarding is you end up living off your reserves. Eventually, you become stale. If you give away

everything you have, you are left with nothing. This forces

you to look, be aware, to replenish... Somehow the more you give away, the more comes back to you."

-Paul Arden

With one sweeping look across the landscape of the world, we can readily see while also noting reasons to be indifferent about extending kindness randomly. Ungrateful receivers, scammers, schemers, and the feeling that your contribution is exponentially disproportionate to the overwhelming presence of lack and need are seemingly good reasons to give nothing else or more.

Generous acts witnessed by others may inspire the onlookers to follow suit and spark an assortment of charitable kindness to quantified levels. We automatically equate giving with money or resources, first. This is a rational go-to; however, we can give our time, release our positive energy, can offer our experience. In some cases, it is the spending of privilege on the outcast, overlooked, and contra-cultural normative communities that is gifted. If greatness is to be attained, excellence is the aim. Greatness is achieved by serving. Social Activist, Brittany Packnett said "The privilege you enjoy comes at someone else's expense. The privilege that you're hoarding could be put to good use.

It could be used to create space, opportunity, resources, and amplification for someone else. Not because they need your saving, but because that is what you do with what you didn't earn. You give it away. So, it's not charity, it's solidarity. True solidarity means showing up respectfully, physically, mentally, and financially. As we grow professionally, our responsibility grows with us so we must spend that privilege, commensurately."

Conversely, we must balance selfless giving and self-care. We can give until it hurts but we shouldn't give to the point that we are harmed.

Providence will cause us to enter some spaces where squeezing and tightening are pervading conditions in order for the dormant and untapped treasure within to be released. "You cannot live a perfect day without doing something for someone who will never be able to repay you. If I give, I will have lived a perfect life" declared John Wooden, legendary former UCLA basketball coach.

Being far removed from giving causes one, by in large, to forfeit receiving. Giving love, granting forgiveness, and showing mercy are concessions that once commended cannot go unpaid. Jesus said "GIVE...and it shall be given unto you..." supply follows sowing. The act of giving grants access to getting. So, then we should look and search out opportunities and search means in which we can better, beautify, and bless others thru our benefaction, not calculating what we have ALREADY done, but making a full impact with what we have freely received.

Prayer:

O God, Giver of every good and perfect gift, I come to you thankful for all the gifts, goodness, and grace that You have sent, send, and will send my way. Help me to discover ways to pour out grace and goodness to others. I want to assist, aid, and add to other people and causes so that Your Light SHINES. I will never forget how good you are to me, Lord. Amen.

Application:

At three points in the day, expresses random acts of kindness.

1. Pick up the tab for a random patron at a restaurant/
2. retailer
3. Give an encouraging word to someone whose path you cross.
4. Spend 10 minutes in a special visit or phone conversation with someone convalescing/homebound/ been a long time since you communicated (classmate or former co-worker)

AFFIRMATION:

MY LIBERAL EXPRESSIONS today are RECOMPENSE IN STORE, TOMORROW.

DO NOT GIVE UP

No matter how long of a good streak one may have experienced, that loathsome LOW LOW day is sure to come. David at the dreaded daunting precipice said so poetically "If I had wings like a dove I would fly away and be at rest." In a very whimsical way, he portrayed and imagined giving up being the satiable ending to a tumultuous ordeal in his life. Situations around you today may seem difficult and dicey! Giving-up should not be your immediate next action! But, Hang-on, help is coming! There is strength on the other side of the struggle. In the gloom, remember you are living FOR THE GOOD.

At some point, we vacillate between taking it on or tapping out, altogether. While reaching for a helping hand, you'll discover that the helping hand is at the end of your own arm. We discover although giving up will effect others, it effects us directly and first.

The presence of a problem is also the beginning of an opportunity to innovate or enhance the quality and standard of life going forward. Scott Barry Hoffman, an NYU psychologist researched creativity for years. He surmises "a lot of people are able to use that (adversity) as the fuel they need to come up with a different perspective on reality....go on to the periphery and see things in a new, fresh light, and that's very conducive to creativity."

Everything may not be alright, but learn to declare and affirm that all is well. Evaluated experience is the best teacher.

Perhaps God has exposed you to this PROBLEM PERPETUALLY UNTIL YOU CAN BE PLEASANT in the PREDICAMENT

Let's pray:

The LORD will mobilize heaven and earth to my rescue this day! I will be made a perfect example of what it is to be blessed, called blessed, and to bless others! I lunge over the opposition with the strategy Yahweh provides. I leap over obstacles with the strength You supply me, God. This is a miraculous day that requires my ALL and cannot tolerate the thoughts of aborting the mission. In Jesus Mighty Name!!! Amen.

Application: (Find three unlikely survivor accounts and describe a main motivation that kept them in until the win)

Person Motivation

1_____. 1._____

_____

2._____. _____

_____

3._____. _____

_____

AFFIRMATION:

I HAVE A TRACK RECORD of BOUNCING BACK & BECOMING BETTER IS A CERTAIN OUTCOME for ME.

YOU HAVE A RIGHT TO LIVE

> *This is how the love of God is revealed to us: God has sent his only Son into the world so that we can live through him.*
>
> *- I John 4:9 CEB*

"Fabre est suae quisque fortunes."

(Every man is the artisan of his own fortune.)

Appius Claudius Caecus (Ancient Roman politician)

Inhale Courage, Exhale Fear. No Matter what anybody says you have the right to be ALL that God created you to be. Connecting to one's organic personhood passed the persona peered upon by the public is a complex undertaking, but with high dividends. The commitment to it is liberating and vital to oneness. German Philosopher Frederiech Nietzsche is quoted as saying "Self-interest is worth as much as the person who has it: it can be worth a great deal, and it can be unworthy and contemptible. Every individual may be scrutinized to see whether he represents the ascending or the descending line of life. Having made that decision, one has a canon for the worth of his self-interest. If he represents the ascending line, then his worth is indeed extraordinary—and for the sake of life as a whole, which takes a step farther through him, the care for his preservation and for the creation of the best conditions for him may even be extreme."

The clarity in your purpose is an inhibitor for discounting who you are. STOP DECLINING THE OPEN CALL to MASTERY considering God PROVIDENTIALLY PLANNED YOUR PRESENCE

Sometimes you have to be bold enough to cut loose some things that got you to where you are but can't go with you to where you're going. If you keep it past its assignment it will hold you back instead of assisting in moving you forward.

Discussion and talks should begin about the PATHOLOGIES of the poor. Simultaneously or concurrently, we NEED to PROBE the PATHOLOGIES of the PRIVILEGED to BREED SUCCESS among MORE PEOPLE EVERYWHERE. For example, Ivy league college students smoke weed, drink alcohol underage, and listen to HIP-HOP music. What contributes to their high success rate, and ability to become working class upper echelon society members? At the top of the list are certainly the grace(s) received as well as good resources. I don't expect government and society to GIVE anybody incessantly; only to be JUST. For, what is granted to one should be granted to the other. Granting SECOND CHANCES to keep the poor out of the courtroom and GRANTING GOOD RESOURCES to the underprivileged students will create more success for the underprivileged as well.

It is easy for people who are stuck without the option to tell you to stay put and play small.

Converse with the CREATOR ON IT. God's purpose for you may be bigger than your dominant gift or ability...

Prayer:

Almighty God, who is the Creator of all life, giver of strength, and Sustainer of my being I can only be because of You. Thank you for stirring me to intentionality and vigor today. Your intervention, infusion, and interaction in my life certify the validity of my human experience. My appreciation to You is best delivered by a determination to LIVE and not merely EXIST thru Your empowerment, embrace, and encouragement, AMEN.

Application (List three things you've survived & three attractive traits about yourself)

_____   _____

_____   _____

_____   _____

AFFIRMATION: I DESERVE TO ENJOY AN ENRICHING EXPERIENCE because THE CREATOR DESIGNATED A SPACE FOR ME TO USE ALL MY SKILLS.

GOING ON FOR OTHER REASONS

You can live through it and outside of it and beyond it One of the reasons that you get up and live each day has to be beyond self- aggrandizement. Getting up and living needs to be traced and tethered, firstly, to an idea, ideal, or individual outside of one's self. If you just get up and live solely because of you, then there will be moments when you will live defeated and in turn, personalize that loss perpetuating defeatism. However, by getting up and living for something greater outside of himself the regard and recognition that one is God-created is a preservative and prompter. Being divinely formed becomes the accouterment for advancement. God made me and that obligates God to sustain me. Provision and protection must come alongside. God made me. A supernatural, superior innovator created me; therefore, it is plausible and possible for the supernatural to frequently accentuate my ordinary terrestrial experience.

The other reason why it is essential to get up and live thru the identification of other reasons extends beyond being God-created to being God-called. There is a greater purpose to self's existence than fulfilling my own desires and things that I want to do.

An effective motivation is that the purpose in me must be shared with the world. The world needs who I am; not just what I have. Not just the gift that I have. Someone needs my vantage, my shared experience, to hear my testimony. I am going because there is a segment of the general population who need to see survival spiting the setbacks. I am going for a benefit that is beyond me. I am going because my skillset is needed. The quotient to the question of relevance to this life comes from motivations that are not sourced to self-promotion. This in no way, negates self-care, nor does it engage a Messianic complex. But it is critical to engagement that identifiable reasons for going supersede YOU. I am going because my children need to see what prudent, upstanding living looks like. I am going to invigorate and add to an organization, partnership, or setting. Jesus said to His disciples "it is expedient that I go, because if I don't go, the Comforter will not come"

Prayer :

Dear Lord, I thank you for a new day that has opportunities peaking from the horizon. Help me today to not sink into despondency but to rise to the occasion of living to my fullest potential so that I can partner with someone who needs inspiration. I want to draw closer to the accomplishment of my aspirations. Thank you in advance for pointing out to me reasons for moving ahead which are passed me. God, I need a divine push and prompting today. Insulate me from apathy. Thank you for creating me, calling me, capacitating me, carrying me, correcting me, and caring for me. Help me to maintain stamina through setbacks, and wherewithal thru woes. Today I set forth thru the empowerment of the indwelling presence of the Holy Spirit to go, glow, grow, and give. Since freely I have received, I reciprocate the gesture so that those who I encounter may be inspired to keep on going, In Jesus' Name, AMEN.

Application:

(list some reasons you are GOING on, today)

_____

—

_____

—

———

———

———

AFFIRMATION:

I PRESS ON KNOWING MY PRESENCE IS A DIFFERENCE MAKER.

I AM THE PROJECT

To put off your old self, which belongs to your former manner of life and is corrupt through deceitful desires, and to be renewed in the spirit of your minds, and to put on the new self, created after the likeness of God in true righteousness and holiness.

- Ephesians 4:22-24 ESV

"It's better to be prepared for an opportunity and not have one-

then to have one and not be prepared"

- Les Brown

Being honest with one's self is a complicated and complexing conversation. For one, appropriately addressing benchmarks and blunders, and even enumerating achievements and egregious downfalls is sure to miscall.

"I could have" is just a fancy way of saying "I am not daring enough" or "I haven't been able to pair my skills to a compatible situation" all of such phraseologies and the like are excuses for doing the painstaking work on "me" so that actualizing the success I am aspiring is realized. Sometimes I am the problem, and that is the reason taking on the project of ME is of incredible significance.

Working on me is often neglected because it appears self-serving and carries less clout than the lofty pursuit of changing the world. When in all actuality, being a world changer is incipient upon transforming MY world. The work I am putting in on myself is not for personal gratification, primarily. It is to make the world a better place beginning with the sphere of influence that I have the greatest control over.

Truth is, my thriving nor my survival, has been predicated on my good decisions, but Divinity's determination to be good to me beyond my poor and proper choices.

Two tools used to pull the potential out of a person are encouragement and shame. There's nothing like shame to shrink the ego and engage a glorious campaign to outshine a failure with a phenomenal feat. AFFLICTION IS used by the ALMIGHTY at times AS AN ATTITUDINAL ADJUSTER.

Healing truly happens when we peal away the labels, and penetrate to deeper layers giving distinctive attention to the pains of the past and the present.

Even when I am the sole believer in my capabilities, it's enough to instantiate great impact as long as I am attuned to my potential. The future me, is depending on the present me to make a difference. And, quite honestly, i can be my own distraction, and trip over myself. When my shoe laces are untied, or if my walk is not the way it should be, then I become complicit in my own denigration and demise. This is why working on ME is of great importance.

It is impossible to respect one's self and neglect self-care. Sometimes people make your CHANGE about them. They do not understand that you've not devalued them to being inadequate in your life. It is simply that you are becoming someone and something that you previously was NOT!

Ponder this interrogative. Will your life be remembered by what the afterlife has gained or by what you left behind? The answer is determined by what we are working to build and that begins inwardly, working outwardly.

Prayer:

Dear God, I come to You humbly and boldly. Boldly, I come because I am Your child, Your workmanship, made in Your image and likeness. I come to you humbly, because all have sinned and come short of the glory. In repentance, I turn to you. As I examine my ways, closely looking at myself; I ask you to improve my ways. I want to live a fruitful life, being a good steward of all things given me and maximizing my life as a Christ follower. In Jesus' Name, Amen.

Application

1. Write all the negative labels put on you by others or yourself.

2. Line thru each of those negative adjectives and descriptions

3. Beside each crossed-out derogatory label, compose a positive adjective that describes who you are.

AFFIRMATION:

I HAVE THE POWER TO CHANGE MYSELF FOR THE BETTER.

WORRY FREE

When my anxieties multiply, your comforting calms me down.

- Psalm 94:19 -CEB

Worry gives small things a big shadow *-a Swedish Proverb* Fear can be accosted thru an approach.

Marcus Tillius Cicero cites six mistakes mankind keeps making century after century:

1. Believing that personal gain is made by crushing others;

2. Worrying about things that cannot be changed or corrected;

3. Insisting that a thing is impossible because we cannot accomplish it;

4. Refusing to set aside trivial preferences;

5. Neglecting development and refinement of the mind;

6. Attempting to compel others to believe and live as we do."

We worry because of loss of control; lack-luster conditions, and corroborative elements that legitimize a conspiracy. Rarely do we get even anywhere close to the reprieve we crave while we are in the crux of unrelentingly stressful and unnerving situations? Partly, this is because we are scurrying about searching our natural spaces for solutions that require a supernatural explanation. Relief from worry is dependent on our reliance in God. We inherently surmise Him to be good all the time; perhaps this is why we are confused when He allows us to suffer, or be involved in an accident or wrongfully accused. Over time we learn that although God is not always good, He is never unfaithful.

We have to let go of the pieces and be set free from frustrations connected to fragments in order to have abiding peace. Many times we are troubled with trouble and quite honestly challenged by triumphs. If we wait out worries they will become wonders in our lives. Worry is like a rocking chair it is powered by energy that doesn't move you forward. Maximize what you are capable of. Give God what you cannot do. Trust God no matter what. Because faith exterminates worry and substantiates worth.

Prayer:

Rock of my Salvation, King of Kings, through days of toil when my heart fails, anchor me through the remembrance of Your faithfulness toward me. Forgive me Lord, for allowing my circumstances and situations to be larger in my view than You. I lift up my eyes to You for help. I want to trust You to tend to every need I have been concentrating on — the physical, financial, relational, social, spiritual, and emotional needs, I know you can provide, refill, and renew. Waves of anxiety will not swallow me. You are my lifeline. You will advocate for me and bring my breakthrough. Thank You for your abiding presence that is with me thru it all. In Jesus' Name, Amen.

Application:

Give all your worries and cares to God, for he cares about you.1 Peter 5:7 - NLT. Divide a sheet of paper into two columns. Title Column One: WORRIES. Above Column Two write: PROMISES. List your worries. Then search the Scriptures for God's promises that should cancel that anxiety.

AFFIRMATION:

I AM SOLUTION DRIVEN. EVERY PLIGHT IS AN OPPORTUNITY FOR GROWTH.

SHOW UP FOR PRACTICE

Do you see a man skillful in his work? He will stand before kings; he will not stand before obscure men.

- Proverbs 22:29 ESV

"If you are persistent, you will get it.

If you are consistent, you will keep it."

~Harvey MacKay

The perception of practice cannot be from a petulant perspective, but must be pursued with a passion for perfection and the prize. The repetitive exertion proves persistency and the resiliency exacted promotes consistency. Showing up for practice is a must. World acclaimed boxer Muhammad Ali "I hated every minute of training, but I said, DON'T QUIT. Suffer now and live the rest of your life as a champion. " Success comes at a residual premium. Perspiration is the necessary saturation to the aspiration. Grecian Philosopher, Aristotle, gave us a contemplation when he weighs in to say "We give up leisure in order that we may have leisure, just as we go to war in order that we may have peace. "

Today may not be the big day, the performance day, or time of recognition, but it is an opportunity to show up for practice. If we we are truly desirous of the prize then we will practice tenaciously. The sweet savor of success does not happen without serious task orientation and seemingly senseless attempts. It is necessary to show up for practice and the times of preparation with the same exuberance and excitement that we show up for performance or to be awarded. One may not have extended to him an invitation to an elaborate, exquisite event. There is a standing invitation to practice developing the skill, the nuances, and simulating adaptations to the unaccounted for sudden popups.

Two driving influencers to the consistency of practice toward perfection are satisfaction and success. Goodly balanced both can stimulate motivation to work toward the end goal. But when feelings of success and satisfaction are irregular, you can be sublimely slothful or miserably magnificent. The trick is to balance satiety and success.

Practice wards off mediocrity and powers our momentum. The more we practice perfectly the more we can adjust the metronome. Nick Sagan, Head Football coach of the University of Alabama who has led the team to multiple national championships in recent years said: "We aren't competing against an opponent necessarily. We're competing against perfection" Many famous people aren't great and many great people aren't famous. Don't be the sad indictment of over-exposure and underdevelopment. Put in the practice that hones skills and develops character and ferocity. Train with the tenacity of an underdog. Present with the passion of an unstoppable force.

Prayer:

God, my Savior & Sustainer, I come to You, believing that with You all things are possible. You specialize in things that seem impossible and great is Your faithfulness. Help me to not become weary in well doing. I need you to hold me through the setbacks and switch-ups and lead me to greater maturity on the other side of it. Empower me to engage in tasks with all my heart and give me the endurance to never lose my heart. Develop in me, consistency and competency, side-by-side. Shield me from shutting down as I believe that this is the way by which I come into being the fullness of who you purposed me to be. In Your Holy Name, I pray, Amen.

Application:

Plan it and set a reminder notification on your phone Match up practice to an existing habit or routine Modify it, if you must BUT GET 'ERR DONE Measure progress by recording it or keeping a record of the results.

AFFIRMATION:

I FEEL COMPLETENESS IN BEING COMMITTED TO FULFILLING MY PURPOSE TODAY I AM SOLD OUT TO BEING MY BEST.

PRAY FIRST

Devote yourselves to prayer with an alert mind and a thankful heart.

- Colossians 4:2 NLT

"But for most of us, the problem is not that we are too eager to ask for wrong things. The problem is that we are not eager enough to ask for the right things"

-Tom Wright

Prayer will make you look beyond personal opinions and cause you to tap into the plan that God has for your life .. so pray and stop worrying about what folks are saying. The journey of life is different when we pray at the start of a new day. God wants you to hear his voice, more than you want him to hear your prayer. Imagine if we gathered for consecration as fast as we gather for controversy.

Arguably, the most profitable discipline of a believer is prayer. There are loads of benefits from a maintained posture of prayer. We are empowered as we seek His face. While we pray, God gives us strategy. When we pray we are emboldened in the wake of conflicts, confidences, and calamity. The greatest benefaction of prayer is that God understands our conveyances and communication, verbal and nonverbal.

Prayer is Devotion to God. Devotion to God through prayer demands that we schedule time for prayer, specifically. Prioritizing time and attention in the presence of the Lord is deserving of a God who graces us to have a growing relationship with Him and provides for us beyond our finite ability.

Prayer is Dependence upon God. We have to shed the inherent feeling that we are autonomous beings. When

I'm conscience, I'm connected. Prayer is a DEFAULT. Attuning ourselves spiritually, obligates us to be intentional about including God's perspective and input in all that we do.

Prayer releases Direction thru God. It is not God's intent for His will to be abstract and nebulous to us. How God proceeds is His prerogative, exclusively. In prayer, God tells us turn-by-turn instructions to arrive at the places He has prepared for us. We are relieved from the burden of computing all the answers and our obedience guarantees good success.

It has well been said that the purpose of prayer is not to get man's will done in heaven, but to get God's will done on Earth. In prayer, our reliance is upon God, entirely. Staying on track with God, and keeping a good outlook happen with consistent communication with the Lord that we call, prayer. We should not pray like we are worrying but instead pray like we are winning. Many times there is nothing wrong with our request, expressly.

But the undenied petition is due to a lack of readiness on the part of the petitioner. We cant ring the bell on heaven's door and then flee like mischievous neighborhood children. We are quick to invite the Lord to speak and simultaneously and just as quickly whisk away taking our interest to listen along with our disappearance.

There is a partnership that exists in prayer that will push you and preserve you.

What is it about this GOD that keeps me talking to Him when it seems like He's not listening .... it's because He's A VERY PRESENT HELP in the TIME of TROUBLE...

A wish is tossed in the air of nothing but a PRAYER is DIRECTED LANGUAGE ADDRESSED to GOD. There are far too many attestations to the effectiveness of prayer to even entertain the thought that it is baseless would be ridiculous.

Prayer:

Lord Jesus, today is your day. I thank You for including me in Your purposes and plans on this day. I acknowledge it is no good of my own. I have in some way failed in my speaking, thinking, and doing. Forgive me. Make me right with You, O God. I need your direction, I seek your instruction. Not only did I desire Your presence with me; but I also recognize how dire I need it. I will not permit my human logic and reasoning to cause me to miss Your voice. I call to you and you promised to answer Lord. Keep me in Your Care, In Jesus Name, Amen.

Application:

Give attention to your posture when praying. Be intentional about it. Consider finding a quiet place in a park to pray while seated on a bench. As you take your morning or evening walk. Turn on soft music in the background. Or, wrap yourself in a scarf. Light a candle. Kneeling beside your bed at night doesn't have to be the only place and way that we offer prayers to God.

AFFIRMATION:

MY PLEA IS HEARD BY GOD & MY HEART IS TUNED INTO the WILL of the LORD.

STUDY THE LOSSES

"But even if you do suffer for doing what is right, you are blessed. Do not fear what they fear, and do not be intimidated"

- 1 Peter 3:14 NRSV

"Never confuse a single defeat with a final defeat."

~F. Scott Fitzgerald

Opportunities are like water they are never lost. Water is always somewhere on land, evaporated in the air as molecules, trapped in a cloud, running in a stream, or collected in the sea... and opportunities missed by one person are capitalized upon by someone ready and hungry. Opportunities never go to waste. Even calamity can become a counselor. Our quest must be to discover dissipating occasions that can be capitalized upon.

Assassinating the aversion to loss is key, to success after a setback.

The time in the test should tabulate into valuable teachings usable on the trek to triumph. It is incredibly important to journal your journey. It was not without hurt. It was not with out hindrance. But fail not to count the help and purpose of what had a completely harmful premise.

There is mercy in blessed subtraction. Don't confuse providence with prerogative. Providence is what GOD divinely orchestrated for you to go through. But some of us are in the fallout of what WE decided and now the repercussions and reverberations we have to now grapple with.

The loss of faith in a disappointing moment delays positioning for what will garner greater in our lives. The courageous teacher feels obligated to pass along the lessons of his failures. The people who want to live in your dream, cannot handle your nightmare. In truth, none of us are standing because we never failed, but rather because we gathered from deep within, strength to get back up.

Don't try to carry the World. Jesus taught "To whom much is given, much is required". It is not to be interpreted to whom much is given ALL is required. The reality is that the anointing doesn't dismantle your humanity. Being gifted doesn't exempt one from the gloom.

Finally, bear in mind that a loss may negate a perfect season but it does not cancel a winning season. To avoid affixation about a bad situation, take an unbiased observation and forthright approach to what is working and that which is broken. Trials embolden, not erase, the convictions of our souls. Consider this, falling is not the end of the world. I wasn't the best husband, but I can still be a good son. I wasn't the best student, but I can still be a life long learner.

Prayer:

Lord of Host, I acknowledge You as Sovereign, Ruler of Everything, a Mender to the Broken and Lifter of my head. I adore you for being my Advocate, Aid, Enabler, Guardian, my Way Out, my Way OVER, my way THRU. I need you to help me in my disappointment. I feel dropped. But, thru given discernment and proper reflection I can extract the lesson, an innovation, and a better strategy going forward. I shake loose feelings of inferiority, insignificance, and impairment. I am not what happened to me. Lord you are restoring me, reviving me, and renewing me even amidst this. You reign forever, so I know though this situation is over my head, it is still under Your feet. It is in Your demographic Lord, it is within your realm of control. Lead me on from this loss to victory, In Jesus Name, AMEN.

Application:

Journal some times when you've received the Lord's mercy.

AFFIRMATION:

I EMPTY MYSELF OF EMBARRASSMENT AS I
EMBRACE IMPROVEMENT

THE STRUGGLE IS REAL

*"He saves me, unharmed, from my struggle, though there are many who
are out to get me."*

- Psalms 55:18

"I thrive on failure. I thrive on things that are not perfect.

It sends me back in the ring to get it right."

-Tom Ford

Sometimes when dealing with problems and attempting
to grapple with them; we personalize the plight.
Affliction has the possibility to alienate us. The familiar

phrase "when the going gets tough, the tough get going" is true. Indeed the path is perilous and taxing. Disappointments and dysfunction will cause tears to roll down your cheeks. Those same cheeks will be raised again once again while striding forward, gleefully.

The first and greatest power wielded through us is sourced to knowing who we are. We cannot lose sense or sight of that during life's turbulent times. Struggle makes existence worthwhile by exposing the expense to simply being. As, Philip Randolph explained, "Justice is never given; it is exacted, and the struggle must be continuous for freedom is never a final act but is a continuously evolving process to higher and higher levels of human, social, economic, political, and religious relationship." When the storm subsides, and it will dissipate, how we made it thru may elude us. The elaboration of details like boisterous winds and the tempestuous stormy blasts will pale in comparison to the remarkable account of survival, emergence, and redemption that your action-packed story relays.

One thing is certain though, a person is altogether different when it is over than just prior to it starting up. If making me better is the struggle's sole purpose, it is completely worthwhile riding out the storm. I got wet. I got worried. But, I didn't get wiped out.

Leaving the place of strength in the process of the scrimmage is a costly error. Heraclitus of Ephesus defined struggle as the father of everything. The struggle relays feedback. Difficulties help us to discover "what is missing?" We are configured to act and input what is meaningful not necessarily what is mainstream. The struggle also helps us in relaying feedback to determine what is malfunctioning. Being married to a methodology can produce disastrous blind spots. The struggle helps us define what is manageable and determine which is meaningful and decide what manner is best.

Articulating an area of weakness really is a freeing experience. Struggling means we are alive. Being in the wringer is a regular position of the cyclical processes in life. It does not instantaneously enact a moratorium against finishing. Nor does it deaden the winner inside of you.

Coming thru is certifiably certain. The struggle is The threat pays a thrill. The threat produces thrive.

The failure to be impactful persists until endorsing the world and interest in influencing change within it becomes entwined. Challenges throughout our lives develop and deepen unconditional love in us, if we allow it.

Prayer:

Lord you are a stronghold for the oppressed, a strong tower in times of trouble. And we who know your name put our trust in you, for you, O Lord, have not forsaken those who seek you. The evil planned against us is foiled. Answer in the day of trouble!

The name of the God of Abraham provides for me! Support with your mighty power. The name of the God of Isaac prospers me! The name of the God of Jacob protects me! Send help from the sanctuary. Insulate us from conflated satanic attack. Many are the afflictions of the righteous, but Lord, you will deliver from them all. In Jesus' Name, AMEN.

Application:

Write down some challenges you are currently facing which are beyond your control. Mark a ✓ besides the ones you have left in the hands of the Lord.

AFFIRMATION:

I WILL KEEP FIGHTING. THE SITUATION IS DIFFICULT BUT I AM SOMEONE WHO IS DYNAMIC.

THE DREAM

"Go confidently in the direction of your dreams, and live the life you've imagined"

-Henry David Thoreau

Dreams, aspirations, and goals are the blueprints for which we lead purpose-filled lives. The impression of your dream is in your mind, and its influence materializes thru your motivations. You can't build what you can't see. Bishop T.D. Jakes said, "If you can see the invisible, you can do the impossible." Dreams are not attained by pessimism or procrastination. The path to the prize is polluted and provocative. Perseverance is necessary. What a beautiful ability it is to dream when you are awake.

Idealism is seeing things as they should be. Vision is seeing things as they SHALL BE. If you are NOT fully persuaded and 110% convinced that there will be major challenges on the way to your dream stage....every failure, negative criticism, betrayal or disappointment will cause you to second-guess every single step of faith that you take.

Everyone has good ideas about your vision. Input will be hurled from the sidelines in the direction of the dreamer by onlookers. These bystanders conveniently seek to reassign and redefine what you have brought from your mind's eye to the visible world.

Don't let anything take your future or cause you to detract and diminish what you've envisioned for yourself. Shortsightedness strips us of the details, descriptions, and dynamics critical to interpreting the whole picture.

An exotic thought without an executional thrust is delusion. But, a dream in motion attracts provision. Anything you desire can be created if you really want it.

The greatest saboteur of the dream stage is irresponsible decisions. Although, we think it is noble, creating responsibilities we cannot fulfill is counterproductive.

Albert Einstein said once that "Imagination is everything. It is the preview of life's coming attractions. I believe wholeheartedly that everyone can ascend to astonishing heights of achievement by keeping a sharp imagination and vigorous inception. Killing another person's aspirations is totally unnecessary for the fulfillment of one's own dreams

Face the fact of being unordinary and embrace that you are outfitted for the EXTRAORDINARY. Making your dream a reality is a process akin to grappling with an awkwardly shaped oversized package. Normalize feelings of complexion and the inner consternation swirling so that you can get over them. It is easy to get discouraged or feel overwhelmed. But, know your purpose and trust your strength. Make it happen. Mold it happily. Mend it heartily.

Prayer:

Lord and Maker of every living thing I know You are in control. You are the Master and Ruler of all. I come to you believing that You have put purpose inside of me. Gifts, skills, and abilities you have equipped me with to live out what You have designed that includes my participation. I thank You, Lord, that as my ways please You, You will give me the desires of my heart. Trusting in You to guide me in making decisions that are aligned with my dreams coming true. Go before me and make the way clear, secure connections that will be needed. Let me grow in stature with God and man. In Your Name, I pray, AMEN.

Application:

Create a vision board of one aspect of your life for short or long term. Place it in an area you frequently visit.

AFFIRMATION:

EVERY DECISION IS TAKING ME IN THE DIRECTION OF MY DREAM LIFE.

BETTER, NOT BITTER

> *"...Make sure that no root of bitterness grows up that might cause trouble and pollute many people."*
>
> *- Hebrews 12:15 CEB*

> *"If I thought about it, I could be bitter, but I don't feel like being bitter. Being bitter makes you immobile, and there's too much that I still want to do."*
>
> *- Richard Pryor*

Being swift to rage defaults to the emotion of anger, and that is an unhealthy preemptive move. Do not let anger be the default mechanism. Bringing resolution to a conflict may require the extension of an olive branch or offering an olive tree. Never should the entire olive orchard be required for reconciliation to commence. There are individuals who put contention on autopilot and thrive from it. People like this will stop at nothing to block pathways to reconciliation to dishevel unity for the continuation of dissension because they profit and gain from the faction.

Jealousy and envy are similar words but do not have the exact same meaning. See, jealousy is when a person is mad at the thought of you having what they have. But, envy is when someone is mad that you have what they don't have. We often equate the words the same because whether an individual or group is envious or jealous they will lie, sabotage, exploit, extort, manipulate, and manufacture if it assures your demise.

Efforts to exclude you shouldn't be surprising when you blow the whistle on deception, decoys, and deceitfulness. It is a common reaction to being exposed. Take it in stride with the exposure of truth.

Sometimes we have mislabeled sicknesses. Revenge is not a passion; it is a disease. Revenge poisons one's soul and perverts one's mind. Payback can be so debilitating. We unknowingly wield our own demise when we incessantly chase what will destroy us from the inside out.

The thing about unhappiness is all it takes is for something worse to happen and you realize it was happiness after all. Maintaining a positive perspective perennially, no matter what is work and requires focused intentionality. The outcome is irreplaceable. Keep this in mind: ripened fruit is the result of good works. Yet, the harvest of bad works is rotten fruit.

PRAYER:

Eternal & Everlasting God I approach the throne of grace knowing I am your beloved. Even though I have been belittled berated, bothered, and busted; Your mercy and grace towards me is the medicine that constricts betrayals, attacks, and lies from becoming bitterness and resentment in me. I appreciate

You, Lord for the unconditional love I receive from you that shields me and reduces the pain I feel when I am assaulted and attacked. I pray you to keep my open wounds and raw hurts from becoming revenge even in my mind. Lord, as Jesus has forgiven us, teach me how to forgive others and bear the fruit of redemption and restoration in every area of my life. In the tender, triumphant and terrific name of Jesus, I pray. AMEN

APPLICATION:

Fill in the Blanks:

Ex: I am a better ___listener__because _I know how it feels being ignored_

Write your own list of at least 10 examples of BEING BETTER I am a better_____ because

_____

AFFIRMATION:

LIGHT SHINES THRU MY CRACKS. THE SCARS ADD VALUE to MY PERSON. I AM GETTING BETTER.

TRUSTING GOD COMPLETELY

"Blessed is the man who trusts in the LORD, whose trust is the LORD. He is like a tree planted by water, that sends out its roots by the stream, and does not fear when heat comes, for its leaves remain green, and is not anxious in the year of drought, for it does not cease to bear fruit."

- Jeremiah 17:7-8 ESV

"Never be afraid to trust an unknown future to a known God."

– Corrie Ten Boom

Truth is in the container of faith. God's prerogative connects to faith and is sure to amaze you. French philosopher, Jesuit Priest, and paleontologist, Pierre Tielhard de Chardin says: "We are not human beings on a spiritual journey. We are spiritual beings on a human journey. " At some point, a person must make a decision, whether right or wrong, and stick to it. The dots cannot be connected looking forward, only from hindsight.

God has already placed encouragers in your path and deposited strength for every challenge that will be faced as the journey through life proceeds. Regardless of how difficult things are or how complex the situation may be, rest in the fact that God went ahead of you to straighten everything out in the end.

There are moments when we requisition and beckon for tangible assurances about our faith. We frequently call for confirmations, maybe not related to the reality of God, as much as the Lord's involvement and intervention in our human affairs. Sign-giving by God is a common motivator used by the Sovereign to attract the trust of God's people. The Lord gave signs thru Moses to Pharaoh and the Egyptians via the ten plagues. The Lord gave signs to Gideon. The Lord gave signs to Hezekiah and Isaiah. God would give signs thru Jesus of Nazareth thru healings, feedings, storm-stallings, and even resurrection. God graciously gives reassuring signs with glorious significance.

Sometimes it is not how strong you can be in the fight, but how strategically you strike back in a scrimmage. The best strategy anywhere is to lock into the plan of God. G.A. Young poeticized the believer's trust in God when penning these words: "Sometimes on the mount where the sun shines so bright, sometimes in the valley, in darkest of night, God leads His dear children along."

PRAYER:

I confess there have been moments when I allowed my own interpretations, insights, and interrogatives to get in the way. My personal observations were weaponized against the outstanding plans you have for me. Lord, I trust You thru the process. Father, I trust You on the path. Almighty one, I trust You to use your power. I come to You because you have a perfect track record of success. There is no failure in You, there is no facade about You, and there is no flaw in You. I cannot trace Your hand, but I trust Your heart concerning me and every aspect of my life, now and even forever.AMEN.

Application:

Write a list of 7 promises God makes to Believers. Recite one each day of the week throughout the day.

AFFIRMATION:

I RELY ON IN THE POWER OF GOD. I CHERISH the PRESENCE of GOD. I FOLLOW the PURPOSE OF YAHWEH because I COMPLETELY TRUST the PLAN of the LORD.

HANDLE BUSINESS

"for they all wanted to frighten us, thinking, "Their hands will drop from the work, and it will not be done." But now, O God, strengthen my hands."

- *Nehemiah 6:9 NRSV*

"Don't sit down and wait for the opportunities to come. Get up and make them."

- *Madam C.J. Walker*

Put sentiments to the side when duty calls. Great companies, civilizations, and personalities have all toppled at the inability to separate personal indulgences from duty. I implore you not to make similar mistakes.

Dispassion is the business person's best friend. One must not get emotionally involved in the business. Listening to the market is critical. What is the market saying? Does it tell of Demand? Does it divulge the commodities' whereabouts? Discerning a message from the times is an invaluable skill set. The Hebrew Bible mentions the sons of Isaachar who were able to discern the times. This gave them a cutting edge on emerging trends and a jump on the concerns which materialize as a result.

Waiting time is not wasted time. But waiting forever is illogical and impossible. The best rebuke to lethargy is movement. Moving forward is impossible when the past is holding us in a chokehold.

Single-tasking is the new super power.

Do not aim to be AVERAGE —strive to be unforgettably AWESOME. They didn't start you so they can't stifle you and certainly, they can't stop you.

The effort you apply instantly today and maintain can be the reversal of prognosis at the follow-up doctor's visit or the next time you check the scale. The effort applied instantly in brushing up the resume or enhancing professional development can be quite rewarding. The spontaneity of effort is amazing. Many times and at various junctures the question is begged "Do you want to come out?" of whatever it is. Apply effort and watch how soon you come out of despondency. Watch how quickly moping turns to merriment. See how soon naysaying and defeatism dissipate and optimism rises. Channel your effort to things that will add to the value of who you are and not take away or denigrate who you are created to be.

Passion and Productivity are Brothers. At success sites, they always rock together and are inseparable. One can not be traded for the other. Once you lose your passion, your productivity will certainly suffer. Stay passionate about whatever you wish to be productive in! Conversely, you can't have a perpetual pep rally. At some point, we must dig in. It may be hard to believe, but know this: God has people in places you have never been praying for you.

PRAYER:

You woke me up this morning and Lord You've started me on my way. These daily engagements are undeniable expressions of endless love & enduring love towards me as well as ALL the children of creation. I invoke Your presence as I go to be a shield for me – that You be the LIFTER of my HEAD. Be my portion of STRENGTH when I get tired today. I purpose to be mature & upstanding in my sayings, doings & goings, THINE IS THE KINGDOM, POWER, & GLORY, FOREVER. Amen.

Application:

Create a personal tagline tweet (140 characters or less) that promotes who you are and your dominant purpose in the world.

AFFIRMATION:

I PUSH THRU. I PULL THRU. I PRESS THRIVE.

BELIEVE IN YOU

Whatever I have, wherever I am, I can make it through anything in the One who makes me who I am.

- Philippians 4:13

" Have the courage to follow your heart and intuition They somehow already know what you truly want to become. Everything else is secondary "

- Steve Jobs

Many avid sports fans, love to watch the games televised, usually. Some fans are loyal to the team and others to their favorite player. For the latter, it means criss crossing with each team the athletic star plays for throughout their career. It is interesting to watch people root for and support athletes and be trapped in feelings of inferiority and self-loathing.

Understandably, it becomes difficult to believe in yourself when your back is against the wall. When there is no readily available aid, no swiftly approaching assistants, or strong and adamant advocacy present, one can quickly liquify from their once strong solid state.

In the wake of the devastation at Ziklag upon their return, the men following King David are upset, and filled with rage. These men were on the edge of accosting David, at the very least. But David, decided to distance himself and was able to achieve centering by encouraging himself in the Lord.

Take some time away from everyone else. Energy drainers detract from investments and deposits that could have been lent to self-development. Connections that are counterproductive contaminate us and conflate reality.

Stop blaming yourself for every situation especially those that you have no control over. Absorbing all of the blame on failed relationships or floundering ventures. Take responsibility rightly. But, self-indictments should be replaced with encouragements.

There is a healthy balance that should keep one from self-aggrandizement and self-absorption that begins with acknowledging our limitations and potential liabilities.

I believe that I can be better. 20th Century Black Liberation Theologian, Howard Thurman, advised "Don't ask what the world needs. Ask what makes you come alive, and go do it. Because what the world needs is people who have come alive."

Each one of us is immature to some extent and this adds to our uniqueness. Our differences are not impediments; they are virtues. If we are looking for disablers and vices we can troll the inventory of abilities for such.

PRAYER:

Lord we thank you for keeping us, carrying us, and caring for us. Flash a signal if I need to be rerouted or am going too fast. Post the green light if I can go for it and help me push out of the park. Today, I believe in ME, only because I was made by you. I affirm that I am beautifully and wonderfully made in Your Divine image, In Jesus Name, AMEN.

Application:

Compose a page of acknowledgments. Who would you acknowledge in your autobiography? Write down the names and reasons why these particular individuals deserve a place in your book and why you are thankful to have crossed paths with them in life.

AFFIRMATION:

ABUNDANT LIVING is MY BIRTHRIGHT and I AM CONFIDENT, DIVINELY MADE, WORTHY, WISE & WONDERFUL.

DO THE RIGHT THING

"Make sure no one repays a wrong with a wrong, but always pursue the good for each other and everyone else."

- I Thessalonians 5:15 CEB

"Knowing what's right doesn't mean much unless you do what's right."

- Theodore Roosevelt

Anyone who has done anything of great significance accomplished it with the assistance of accomplices.

You have the Creator with you. Advocacy of the Almighty comes with God's companionship. He formed and fashioned each of us. We inherently arrived in our human experience equipped with

We have Him in both transcendence & eminence

If God be for us, who can be against us?

You have the Collaborators. God has strategically placed persons around you to get it done.

Discomfort is where growth starts. Revving up Discipline, dedication, determination; and drive will definitely take you places!

I have the motivation to Get UP & LIVE because you

Doing the right thing will cause you to stumble up on blessings. Laurels and laudable expressions of gratitude and admiration for noble actions may not be thrown in your direction. So many zealots pick a side or cling instead to some ideology by which to interpret the world. But, to arise each new day and engage in the arduous task of deciding what to believe, discerning what is right today, and dissecting when to stand up or sit down truly does take courage.

Doing the right thing for the wrong reasons In many ways, we are conduits or bridges. Our purpose at certain junctures along life's journey is solely to connect an individual to someone else. When we function as such we painfully witness the revolving door. This can onset Your feelings of loneliness, being used, and discarded. But do not let these aforementioned feelings rest in your thoughts or heart. Be grateful for the opportunity to teach, impart and invest in someone else's betterment. Remember, what you make happen for someone else God will make happen for you.

Prayer:

Righteous God who is faithful and true in your judgments. I thank you for an audience with you; that you hear me when I call and listen when I pray. Lord, remove the feelings of pressure sourced to the size of my encumbrances and relieve me from the guilt connected to my errors. Thank you for disconnections from the wrong people and connections to the right people. I am grateful to You, Lord for bestowing to me blessed grace & extending new mercy usward. I need a spirit of wisdom and divine steering to make the decisions that best represent You on earth. I want to be right, I want to be clean. I got to be whole. In the Precious, Powerful, and Preeminent Name of the Prince of Peace, Jesus Christ, I pray, solemnly, AMEN.

Application:

Take a sheet of paper and identify 5 recent personal moral situations. Reflect honestly on your response, actions, and recourse. Then, rate your moral motivation (the willingness to do the right thing regardless of the consequences) for each one separately. Add the total and divide by five for your mean average to your personal motivation.

AFFIRMATION:

IT FEELS GOOD TO DO GOOD. THE REWARD IS NOT IN APPLAUSE BUT BEING ABLE TO LIVE WITH THE CHOICES I MAKE.

UNIQUELY YOU

You made all the delicate, inner parts of my body and knit me together in my mother's womb. Thank you for making me so wonderfully complex! Your workmanship is marvelous-how well I know it.

- Psalm 139:13-14 NLT

"It takes courage to grow up and become who you really are."

-E.E. Cummings

Life presents us an opportunity to truly unravel who we are thru the exploration of self. Knowing how one's own feelings, ideas, and principles shape their actions in different situations is what's meant by "self-awareness." The ability to know oneself intimately, flaws and all, and to have a strong feeling of self-assurance and direction in life. Yes, parents or guardians at birth give us a name.

And, during childhood, it is not uncommon to even be tagged with a nickname. How one intimately and indiscriminately explores one's self bears significance to one's life experiences. For example, being unacquainted with personal vulnerabilities could lead a person to feel victimized at the slightest challenge. How we experience ourselves effects how we express ourselves.

Our perspective is predominantly predicated on our perception. At some point, one must come to this determination "I am okay with NOT being normal." Some may mistake originality for an oddity. I am not a freak of nature, although my composition is a phenomenon. I am an exceptional being. You and I were born lacking nothing however, we must submit to environments that consistently activate and affirms what God put inside. Do not dilute indescribable and some time raw quality by being subjected to normalization.

Who says you can't optimize the multifaceted person you are to be? Divinely designed, is it unfathomable to become a history-making, game-changing, record-breaking specimen? Only the person who is not acquainted with you, entirely, would assert such a supposition. Your pundits many times have only stepped into a segment of your journey and have no clue of the other abilities you possess or prowess you may hold which make you an asset. The Late Bishop Kenneth Moales, Sr said "What you are is an opinion... who you are is a revelation!"

Have you restricted your potential by giving too much validity to other people's opinions of you? Don't be a wanna be; be who you want to be. Because the cure for rejection is identity. A freed self in existence is a soul fully living. A freed self cannot coexist in a comparison-framed mentality. God didn't equip you with what they have, because you've been divinely gifted with something else they don't possess. Discover value and victory from within. You weren't placed in this world to primarily conform but to catalyze events, environments, and engagements. Impact and improvement should be the result of your involvement as your authentic personhood.

Each one of us is immature to some extent and this adds to our uniqueness. Our differences are not impediments; they are virtues. If we are looking for disablers and vices we can troll the inventory of abilities for such.

At times we are subject to dim our shine so that others will feel comfortable in our presence. Apologizing for who you are is a global let down. It is nearly impossible to enjoy life with considerable self-abhorrence.

PRAYER:

God, we receive Your love and affirm our identities in You. Grant us the bravery to be bold witnesses of your goodness in a world up-wrought. May Your strength be made known even in our weaknesses so that we can be the image of Christ that this world needs. Amen.

Application:

Plant a "WHO AM I?" Tree

1. Trace your hand on the paper with your fingertips open to make longer branches.

2. Draw branches with plenty of leaves from your fingertips.

3. Create as many leaves as you wish (make them large enough to write or draw within!)

4. Sketch dirt with a line across the base of the tree allowing space for writing or sketching at the bottom of the page.

Each segment of the tree is a different area of reflection. The **SOIL** represents: "**I'm supported...**" Consider your supporters; those who have cultivated courage and kindness in you. Write them in the soil

The **TREE TRUNK & BRANCHES** represent: **I'm GLAD...**

Beginning at the bottom of the tree and working your way up through the branches, reflect on the places, things, and experiences you are grateful for (e.g., my family, friends, doctors that help me feel better when sick, the school where I meet my friends, the outdoors where I can exercise and see new things).

Finally, the **LEAVES** represent: **I AM/ I LOVE** Identify your unique qualities. They may be adjectives (funny, clever, kind, helpful, wonderful friend, etc.) or your favorite activities and interests (playing soccer, painting, dancing with grandpa, mastering arithmetic).

AFFIRMATION:

I AM UNORDINARY and UNBOUND from NORMS to the UNFATHOMABLE. I AM A WHOLE VIBE.

THE GIFT OF NOW

Besides this, you know what time it is, how it is now the moment for you to wake from sleep. For salvation is nearer to us now than when we became believers;

- Romans 13:11 NRSV

"Beware the barrenness of a busy life."

- Socrates

Time keeps moving right along. We have a tendency to miss progression falling prey to depression from unfulfilled expectations, oppression by nostalgic intoxication, and suppression by inactivity. This regretfully occurs when we counted on more time or a more ideal space. Reflect on yesterday and be ready for tomorrow, hopefully. But, do not allow either contemplation to subtract from the present destiny moment or detract from the responsibility to manage the "now" moment.

The gift of now is tempered and solemnized by confronting real problems and responding in the most appropriate manner.

One of the greatest favors we can do for ourselves is to take advantage of the availability. Perfectionism is the first cousin of procrastination. Both bring traction and gravitational pull against ascending toward actualizing our ambitions and goals. But when we make a move, the Master makes a way!

There is an ancient story about six blind men who are all brought to meet an elephant. "It's very much like a wall", declared the first man as he touched the elephant's tough dry skin. It is spear-like, said the second man as he felt the elephant's tusk. Then, the third man, gripping the elephant's hosing trunk said, "It is so much like a snake!"

While the trunk squirmed like a worm in his grasp. No! No! No! You've all got it wrong!" exclaims the fourth man. Wrapping his arms and legs around one of the beast's legs he cries " this animal is so very similar to a tree." The fifth man stretching and pulling on the elephant's ear remarked how easy it is to know that this beast is like a fan. Finally, the sixth man, grabbing the tail confidently proclaims "the elephant is just like a rope." One compelling interpretation from this story is that we all have a piece of reality, that is too vast to contextualize, compartmentalize or comprehend in one moment in time. Reality requires exploration. Deep exploration. We cannot appreciate it with one sense alone. Do not limit reality's expression to what you feel from it...Hear what reality speaks. Taste what reality dishes, See what reality displays now, smell ....Extensively coalesce, and engage with the facts of existence. Be bold enough to burst your bubble and step outside of your individual experience to be observant of what others' reality is and make a legitimate effort to empathize.

The truth is often so elusive and often imaginary. In the end, however, it is all we have left.

A sign of mishandling an assignment is inconsistency. Being caught up and overwhelmed with unsureness will be the root cause of mismanaging a moment. Never assume that it will come around again. Stop second-guessing and gratefully own this now moment that you have.

PRAYER:

Almighty God, Author and Finisher of our Faith; from everlasting to everlasting You are God. You are gracious. You are Great. Contemplation of your greatness, Lord, reminds me of where I have missed the mark toward you. Whether in word thought or deed by acts of commission or omission, I pray that you would pardon me and blot out my transgression, purify me, and make me new. I thank you for incorporating me into your purposes and plans for this day. It is a time that I have never seen, nor will I see again. Lord help me to make the best of the time I have. Help me with precision and proficiency. Give me strategies around time-wasting. I praise you for hearing my prayers, petitions, and pleas as well as receiving my praise.

Application:
 WHAT AM I DOING?

Time yourself - Allocate say 25 minutes to completion of a bite-sized task.

Track yourself -Analyze whether you hit the target time
Treat yourself- Award yourself every time you beat the goal.

AFFIRMATION:

THE NOW THAT I HAVE WILL NOT GO WASTED.

THRU THE PAIN

> *"...You will have pain but your pain will turn into joy."*
>
> *- John 16:20*

> *"Out of suffering have emerged the strongest souls; the most massive characters are seared with scars."*
>
> *-Khalil Gibran*

Vulnerability emits both an awesome and destructive power. Much of the pain we deal with is the passport to promotion.

Newt Gingrich, a famous late 20th-century politician said "Perseverance is the hard work you do after you get tired of doing the hard work you already did."

Pour up enough memory and we can drown misery into a watery grave. Play symphonic syncopated sounds allowing each complicated note to include the dissonance to empower a dance in the rain instead of resorting to sitting and sulking with the soundtrack of melancholy melodic ballads surrounding.

Attacks against You

In the birth story of Jesus Christ, Herod wants to find Jesus to kill Him. He doesn't want to wait until the Christ child has become an adult, but to annihilate him in his infancy. While you may not feel that you are a threat to someone else's progression; others can often pinpoint the trajectory of your potentiality. Out of fear that you will overshadow them, these persons are apt to kill your character and vandalize your vision. But don't get bogged down in their battles, business, or befuddling when you know you must be about your business.

Some of us think our lives are a vial of tears. Pain can be like a loan, except no matter what you do clearing the indebtiture is seemingly impossible. Know this, where others hurt you, God and time will heal you.

The burden of power can be painful. In this instance, being vigilant and resolute is necessary.

William Shakespeare's Julius Caesar is quoted as saying: "It is easier to find men who will volunteer to die than those who are willing to endure pain with patience." As hard as it is to feel pain it is more harmful to be void of sensory irritations, numbness, and ineptness to the sensation of the hurt.

Our most difficult moments are in many cases, the most defining moments. So feel the pain, feel the loss and injury. Then turn those feelings into fuel and make forward motions. Remember mourning introduces the morning.

PRAYER:

Lord of the HEAVENS & LORD of HERE we the offspring of creation THANK YOU for ANOTHER DAY to LIVE BETTER & SHINE BRIGHTER. Shape us more in the

IMAGO DEI. Shake from our insecurity, irritability & most of all iniquity. We cherish Your presence that helps in every way. God, without You being near we would be hopelessly void of a way at all. You will be made plain to us, thru us, and even in spite of us-In the Name of God who is LOVE, the Son of God who personifies SACRIFICIAL LOVE, and the Spirit of God that incarnates the world with LOVE, AMEN.

Application: A WORRY DATE

Setting a "worry date" is one method for coping with this anxiety. Allocate approximately 30 minutes 2-3 times a week to fret. Take 10 to 15 minutes on this date to write down what is bothersome to you.

AFFIRMATION:

MY SUFFERING SUPPLIES STRENGTH. SILENCE FOR
ME IS SACRED.

RESULTS MATTER

"Yet we hear that some of you are living idle lives, refusing to work and meddling in other people's business. We command such people and urge them in the name of the Lord Jesus Christ to settle down and work to earn their own living."

- 2 Thessalonians 3:11-12 NLT

"Happiness does not come from doing easy work but from the afterglow of satisfaction that comes after the achievement of a difficult task that demanded our best."

~ Theodore Isaac Rubin

Periodically we will face what are seemingly insurmountable challenges, the type that arouses anxiety even at the shadow cast by the tremendous problem.

Our actions can destroy the world created by our articulations. It is possible to design a world with one's mouth only for it to be destroyed with contradistinctive movements.

Progress and production proceed with patience in the process. Being taken seriously requires consistent execution. No one can be the fruit and the seed at the same time. Neither can he be the tree and seed simultaneously. Long-standing great expectation brings us great things. Great things happen when we least expect them and when we are geared up to execute to an aspired end.

Affixation to idealism is an insidious way to mentally escape from your goal. Because perfectionism calls off just as many projects as pessimism and procrastination do. Work with what you have until it becomes more or you are blessed with more.

At some point, a line must be drawn in the sand. If we are to approach advancement and make achievements we must abandon the inclination to exclusively deal with the exterior shell and neglect infrastructure. Before the Property Brothers, or Chip & Diane who star on Home & Garden Television Network shows, there was Bob Vila. Bob Vila would renovate and rehabilitate homes. Before the visible cosmetic finishes and aesthetics were bettered the investigation of the infrastructure would ensue. Tearing out walls or ensuring electricity circuits were up to code and even double checking plumbing before beautiful vanities and sinks were installed were priorities Mr. Vila took great care ensuring they were up to code.

Value is released thru versatility.

An often overlooked consideration, yet typical tragedy in war is the underestimation of how formidable the enemy is. Sometimes it is not how strong you can be in the fight, but how strategically you strikes back in the scuffle. The right move will make the giants fall. Since, HOW we win matters as much as HAVING the win.

Attainment is the bottleneck to advancement. Your results won't matter to everyone else. But, the results are for you.

Venerable.Verifiable.Valuable. Results give you creditworthiness in society and self-comfort.

When a student is matriculating thru a program of studies, the completion of the task or concept is necessary to successfully carry out the assignment. Passing the class is hinged on being able to repeatedly complete tasks, finish assignments, and master the final exam. Earning a bachelor, master, or doctoral degree can be stopped if the student is not focused on the assignment.

This action of finishing compounds and builds a positive future.

Jesus tells the story of two men who build homes. One man builds his house on the sand. No doubt, it shortened the build time to do so. He estimated that no one would see the foundation so then it could be foregone. Think about it, no one visits your home and remarks "Oh what a beautiful foundation your home has". But not having a proper foundation puts the structure, in its entirety, at risk. The beautiful cabinetry, the lovely hardwood flooring, and any other decorative appointments become irrelevant when the foundation gives way. The other man who built his house

PRAYER:

God, You are my strength and my hope. Lead and guide my thoughts, decisions, and actions today. Grant me the strength to accomplish my goals for the day and help me be gracious to myself if I don't. Let others experience the inexhaustible love you show me daily. Protect us and cover us. In Jesus' Strong Name, I pray, AMEN.

Application: WHAT³

In this exercise you will make three lists of what's, hence the title What cubed…

1. **WHAT is working?**

2. **WHAT is NOT working?**

3. **WHAT is missing?**

AFFIRMATION:

MOVING IN FAITH PLUS MAINTAINING FOCUS EQUALS MANIFESTING FRUIT

WITH PURPOSE IN MIND

The purposes in the human mind are like deep water, but the sintelligent will draw them out.

- Proverbs 20:5 NRSV

"A thing is might big when time and distance cannot shrink it"

- Zora Neale Hurston

MY SIGNIFICANCE is LINKED more to "WHY I am " than "who I am" Take care to not confuse passion with calling. Passion is what one enjoys doing while calling is what he was created by God to do!

Appointed time has less to do with your performance and everything to do with a purpose released in a set time.

"No matter what he does, every person on Earth plays a central role in the history of the world. And normally he doesn't know it ." ~Paulo Coelho THE ALCHEMIST

History proves that multitudes will flock and follow a man who at least knows where he is going. Frustration surfaces in life as people want to use your momentum to control the direction. As is the practice of advertisers when they use the phraseology of "fastest growing" and "best selling".

A fruitful life is the end result of deliberate work that is unwavering and focused.

A focused life is fueled by the discovery of God's will for his life. The enlightenment emanating from understanding the will of God gives incite to the incidents of our lives that transport us along the way He has designed which inevitably drops us off at the point of destiny.

Complacency is an enemy to the completion and execution of purpose. It stems from latent abhorrence or apathy. It is possible to encounter so much conflict all at once that one throws both hands up and the attitude becomes "I DON'T CARE, ANYMORE". Relinquishing and resignation are often called complacency. One of the greatest inhibitors of success is not failure, but boredom.

Should the path be obstructed, rework a new route or obtain a different mode of transportation, but never change the destination. Perfect peace is possible in plighted predicaments when the concentration and focus are on production possibilities for working purposes.

What is produced from putting work into one's purpose is legacy and longevity.

The world is a Jumbotron simulcast of lectures, lessons, and capstones teaching us about opportunities. In some moments we learn to create them. Other times we are taught to cultivate opportunities. We are also taught to kill them. No matter where we are in time, temperament, or location our "WHY" does not lose raised relevance.

PRAYER:

God, Your Word promises me that by seeking first Your reign over my life that I will be led to a life of blessing, purpose, and freedom. I know that I belong to You. Help me to follow your priorities, furnish your passion to those I meet today, and make Your name great. As I focus on Your agenda, Lord, I know that justice and joy will surface around me. I pray this earnestly in your Eternal and Efficacious name of Immanuel, AMEN.

Application:

Imagine you have won a 90 million jackpot prize. You never have to work again, resources are far from limited and the restraints on your time are lifted. Answer the following prompts:

What will your life be like in one month, one year, and 10 years?

How and why would you spend your time (what would a typical Tuesday look like)?

What value will you provide others? Which of your abilities, skills, and insights would you use and develop?

What would be the most uplifting and proud-inspiring inscription that the Ultimate version of yourself, your Hero, would have engraved on their tombstone?

AFFIRMATION:

I AM PAYING ATTENTION TO WHAT BUILDS PURPOSE, BRINGS PROFITS, AND

BIRTHS PEACE. I AM PARTNERING WITH THOSE WHO CAN HELP ME BRING PROFITS, PEACE, & PURPOSE.

PROTECT YOUR PROGRESS

The builders built with swords fastened in their belts, and the trumpeter stayed by my side.

- Nehemiah 4:18 CEB

Hard work beats talent if talent doesn't work hard

-Tim Notke

Protect the progress of personal development, vocational life, as well as relationship constructs. However far along in the journey that a person finds himself, you have come too far to allow adversaries, hardships, hindrances, or hurdles to obstruct, eat away, or erode what you have accomplished. It becomes incumbent upon one to develop a strategy to protect progress.

One of the best tributes to how far you've come is to continue striving farther and higher. It is agitating and disconcerting to listen to someone harp on their successes of a decade ago with no recent successes. It brings on the expression and reaction of a boy who has to constantly listen to his forty-something-year-old father tell stories of his high school football days while playing catch, traveling on a family vacation, and at every holiday feast. Our achievements have expirations too. This is why continuous improvement must be a part of our regular regimen.

The second strategy to protect progress is improvisation. In making the next moves, you won't know everything to do, per se. But what you are equipped with is enough context clues to improvise in the meanwhile until a more clarified plan from God becomes visible. Without all the background information, statistics, or research but there is enough available to continue to thrive

A third strategy to protect your progress is enthusiasm. Henry Ford is quoted saying "Enthusiasm is the yeast that makes your hopes shine to the stars." Enthusiasm is like laughing gas in that you are medicated to laugh thru the pain. Enthusiasm thru the dental surgical procedure makes it more palatable. In many instances, we have left our progress far too vulnerable because our enthusiasm deflated too quickly. The long-term strategy should not be sacrificed or traded for bite-sized, short-term success.

A final impetus to protecting your progress is innovation. Innovation is not imitation. It is possible for our own ambitions and desires to be at odds with our current production. But, we must not allow the old versions of ourselves to mess up the now purpose that we are to live out. Meticulous design and maintainable deployment are crucial elements when the possibilities of increased proficiency and insulated yields are at stake. Great ideas are like Spartan athletes. They are enamoring, efficient, and energetic. Both arouse celebration and the death of either evokes sorrow.

Nehemiah was a builder, restorer for Israel, and the catalyst to a renaissance of the former glory of the nation-state. But Nehemiah's passion alone would not get the fortified walls up nor the city rebuilt. He found a remnant group that shared his passion for rebuilding. Nehemiah instructed them to put a brick in one hand and a sword in the other. Powerful imagery this is. We need a mind to do great things. We need materials to do great things. And we need a defensive mechanism to protect what we have accomplished. In the process, you may very well be characterized as a monster. Anyone who does, however, is mistaken. Where your progress is concerned in certain instances it is a must that you roar and in sparse moments even get ratchet to get where you need to be and fend for what you have with tears, sweat, and blood, built. Let no one make you repent for that.

PRAYER:

Lord Almighty, our Strength & Shield, The Way, The Truth, and The Life I come before you as humble as I know how. Dear Lord forgive me for falling short in word, thought, or deed, by acts of omission or commission. I know and realize that in comparison to Your Divine Splendor, I am but a speck. I can do some things but You, O God, can do all things short of failing or being false. Praying to You, God, to strengthen the works of my hands. Enable me. Empower me. Give me a spirit of wisdom to protect the progress in life You have graced me to make. Enhance my discernment and decision-making abilities. Take me all the way, I pray, In Jesus' Name, Amen.

AFFIRMATION:

I AM CONSCIOUS OF MY PURPOSE. GROWING COMPLACENT IS NOT MY GAME PLAN. I AM COMMITTED TO MY PERSONAL GROWTH.

YOU GOT THIS

1st to be stronger than your feelings.

We do not become what we point to, pick on, or pick out but what we are persuaded of. Our persuasions or convictions are conferred by what we read, who we listen to, and the environments we set ourselves around. Oppressive and claustrophobic environments lack the ventilation and breathing space to blossom and develop. Abusive negative voices have the tendency to retard our progress and can be counterproductive. Alice Walker said, "The most common way people give up their power is by thinking they don't have any." The venues we are located in and the voices we listen to as well as other factors have the power to influence us that we indeed are powerless. Conversely, with encouragement, a conducive learning environment and space to fail our strengths are amplified. This sets us up for life success.

Believing requisites being deliberate. Action gives trust to its constitution. Paranoia and panic are removed because God's presence reveals there is a way OUT. Commitment requires the correct utilization of opportunity cost evaluation. It shows whether what is being done is futile or fruit-bearing.

The knowledge of who you are will enable you to refrain from defining yourself by the circumstances you are in. The circumstances will change. There will be challenges, triumphs, storms, and sunny days. The journey will have uphills and downfalls. The combination of being forward and flexible is critical to withstand life's fluctuations. You've gotta do it pedestaled in shining moments and pitted in shame at other times.

Failures in hard times are certainly inopportune and the bruises are not tattoos, since they are temporary. Falling is inevitable, too. But, Grace is available. Get up like America's President Bill Clinton. Clinton's second presidential term was pervasive with controversy as he was involved in an extramarital affair. He has outlived that scandal and remains a well-respected former president in the present day. Get up like the 46th President, Joseph Biden who after two unsuccessful runs for the highest office in America during the 1988 and 2008 election cycles won the popular vote by over 5 million American voters and displaced the incumbent President, Donald J. Trump.

What you are waiting to come to you has always been in you. One's beginning becomes their being. The beginning is where life starts. Becoming is what life seeks. Being is where life settles. Bravery is in the heart of every man. One day, someday it will be summoned and you must step forward and shine. Be brave enough to envision exponentially. Thomas Merton a Trappist monk once stated: "The biggest human temptation is to settle for too little" So, don't settle for a little when you can strive for a lot.

Prayer:

Living Lord, in Your word I am instructed and invited to pour out my heart to You. I am assured that I can cast my cares upon You since You care so endearingly for me. You are my refuge, and I know anything I fathom or feel is safe in Your keeping. Since you are my safe place, I bring you my hesitations, frustrations, and concerns about making it. I bring You Lord what is delighting me, what is discouraging me. I can speak to you about what I desire and what I am slow to try. Help me and guide me in every area. Strengthen my self-image and self-esteem to a sober level where I truly embrace being able to do all things thru You, God, who strengthens me. I love you today for lifting me. In Your Holy and Hallowed Name, I pray, AMEN.

Application:

Do you believe God has called and commissioned you for a task that you are hesitant to begin?

Reflect on What you might be afraid of?

Next, reflect on What the worst is that could happen? Finish the reflection by identifying what's the best that could happen.

AFFIRMATION:

I HAVE BEEN WORKING TOO HARD FINDING MYSELF, FREEING MYSELF, and FORGIVING MYSELF TO EVER FORFEIT ME, AGAIN.

FLOW

Being enlivened in the early setting of this new day I could hear as clear as the crisp clasp of a cold Cola can opening "FLOW" like a command in my ear.

My connection to FLOW attracted me to the time in John's gospel when Jesus stood and said something about FLOW

In John, Jesus takes on the maternal roles of birthing and nurturing. When explaining to Nicodemus about being born again; water, womb, and Spirit are presented. As the feast of Tabernacles concludes in Jerusalem JESUS stands and borrows the Judean prophetic reference:

"Just as the Scripture said: 'streams of living water (hydor zōn) will FLOW out of his (autos) womb/belly (koilia)." [I should note we do have difficulty with the Greek translation here]

So again we see the repeated theme of water, womb & Spirit. And we will see it again if we look in the delivery room of Golgotha when Jesus births the church without an epidural at Calvary. Mary of Nazareth who birthed him is standing as the attending midwife.

In John 7:37-39 Jesus was speaking of the Holy Spirit who would come to the front actively in the not too distant future. John loved to show throughout his account the clairvoyant, supernatural ability of Jesus to know things & to make prognostications.

The FLOW of water in child birthing we term as her "water breaking" is characterized by a pressurized GUSH like water from a hydrant.

The FLOW of water in birthing also connotes the path out. When that amniotic sac ruptures the water that was in now goes out. In Genesis the Spirit is brooding over the water —hovering, the inference is like mating dancing. In John, the Spirit is actively out. Though, he doesn't let us get ahead of the story, reminding his post-resurrection audience of the sequence of events.

THE FLOW of water also signals delivery. The water — LIVING WATER is present for the development of the church, in utero; to the delivery of the church & later the designation as the church.

The question would come in Acts "Have you received the Holy Spirit since you believed?"

Today we FLOW - in the power of the Spirit releasing pressure for new life & new births

Today we FLOW- in the path, Spirit has revealed for Divine manifestation

Today we FLOW - the promise from the Spirit can be received by all who believe.

Prayer:

Son of God who has set me free and Truth who makes me free, I thank you for causing me to live and capacitating me to breathe. You are the air that I breathe and the source of all life. As one of the children of creation, I call for Divine Help to assist me in unbinding the Gospel and unwinding myself. I want to freely render worship and praise to Your name and flow without hesitation into the life You have designed for me. Great is Your faithfulness and I want to be more faithful to You by yielding to the Spirit in all that I am and all that I have. In the Loving, Lifegiving, and Liberating name of Christ, The Lord, I pray, AMEN.

AFFIRMATION:

I WILL WALK IN FREEDOM. I WILL WALK IN FUNCTION. I WILL FLOW & FLOURISH FROM BEING FAITHFUL

Application:

Locate a local streaming body of water, a creek, a river, or even the beach to visit. The objective is to pay attention to the pattern of the water's movement, its path, and the natural power it represents. Contemplate ways you can allow the Spirit to work in your life.

WHEN IT DOESN'T SEEM FAIR

Here is something else I have learned: The fastest runners and the greatest heroes don't always win races and battles. Wisdom, intelligence, and skill don't always make you healthy, rich, or popular. We each have our own share of misfortune.

- Ecclesiastes 9:11 CEV

"Each day is a special gift from God, and while life may not always be fair, you must never allow the pains, hurdles, and handicaps of the moment to poison your attitude and plans for yourself and your future."

-Og Mandino

"Why me?" is the question that surfaces when disruptive and destructive events suddenly impact our lives without our direct or indirect causation. What bears reflection is how affliction has a way of appraising

ABILITY and AMBITION. After being leveled out, the only thing left to do is level up and be lifted up. Exposure to the gamete of interactions; whether good, bad, indifferent, or ugly along life's journey leads us right back to the ONE who sent us.

Our character is developed in the grind of everyday life. In the crossroad of decision-making lies the pondering of why can't things be smoother. Or, things could be simpler? Even the handpicked have to deal with hardship, and a bad hand can be your greatest weapon. When there is no hope you can bluff magnificently. Or, tap into your hope and expectation of the ending superseding the beginning.

Limitations or liabilities are the obstacle course which allows one to prove their legitimacy. So, caution must be taken in overvaluing the situation or circumstance we are going thru. When we do we underestimate the God, grit, and greatness within.

Managing feelings of unfairness is possible. One strategy is to replace frequent interjections with more personal introspection and reflection. Sensitivity to time and place is paramount. Most times the outburst is not going to get us to the desired outcome. Even when others around you may incite you to do so, don't speak out of turn or utter words that may be regretted later.

Another skill beneficial in Depend on Balance Detainment is not denial. What is due has to be delivered inevitably. It is awe-inspiring how the Master can move marvelously even in messy situations.

Dark clouds rolling in threaten an outdoor event with cancellation. But, one thing to remember cloud cover over the landscape at an aerial view doesn't stop the progress from happening at the ground level. Problems don't stop me from progressing Situations don't stop me from being successful.

Hardship doesn't respect topography, geography, or anatomy. The austerities of life help us learn to live with a very fluid and flexible definition of *okay*. So, be careful in low moments not to erase your experience because of unmet expectations. Life will always be unfair if we complain about it without ever doing any corrective action.

Prayer:

God you are the source of hope, even in worrisome circumstances. You are the center of my joy and bring peace to me as I closely cling to You in faith. I feel my hope is growing through the indwelling presence and power of the Holy Spirit. By Your Spirit, Lord, my feelings of being defenseless are dispelled. I believe that you are with me so I will not allow the tempest to terrify me. I appreciate You O God for protecting me amidst dangers visible and those that were veiled. I adore you for being forever faithful in saving me and acknowledging my desperate cries. In the Precious, Powerful, and Providential Name of the Prince of Peace, Jesus Christ, AMEN.

AFFIRMATION:

MY JOURNEY IS DIFFERENT AND AT TIMES, IS DIFFICULT. BUT, A JOYFUL DESTINY AWAITS.

Application:

Develop contentment by identifying the good in the current events of our lives. This can be achieved by:

—Journaling three things I am thankful for each day — Telling someone about a HIGH of the day

—Celebrating accomplishments PROMPTLY.

COUNT IT ALL GOOD

"Indeed we count them blessed who endure. You have heard of the perseverance of Job and seen the end intended by the Lord — that the Lord is very compassionate and merciful."

- James 5:11 NKJV

When you're going through a tough spell, it's easy to think that's all your life is about. You forget the good things, forget the quiet places. But, they're always inside of us and we can pull them up when we need to set ourselves right.

~ Joan Bauer

An accurate composite reflection would reveal out of all the crescendos and crashes it all really does average out. Strength is not measured by what one possesses. Strength surfaces from what you have handled. Trials will strengthen personal convictions and for the faithful trouble will straighten the convictions of God's presence, purpose, and power within our lives.

Jesus Christ's exhaustive fight at GETHSEMANE is what set the stage for the FLAWLESS experience at

GOLGOTHA. The crucial scrimmages and conflicts are concealed, and the visible conflicts are merely the consequential ricocheting of the inward combat.

Faster-paced personal progress is presented as one operates at some level of pain even that which we have counted as most unbearable. When our life feels like it is falling apart it doesn't matter where we are. It can be difficult and almost unfathomable to perceive, but an accident or even an incident can become a fortunate event.

Opportunity is an overlooked element in our day and an underutilized tool on daunting days. The world is a

Jumbotron simulcast of lectures, lessons, and capstones teaching us about opportunities. In some moments we learn to create them. Other times we are taught to cultivate opportunities. We are also taught to kill them.

Some of the CONFLICTS that we encounter BRINGS parties in the relationship CLOSER or CLOSURE. Confrontation doesn't have to mean CONSTERNATION, automatically.

Whoever counted you OUT, obviously cannot COUNT. To be taken for granted is a compliment. It means I am reliable, and dependable. It says I am consistent and persistent. There is unspoken confidence that I can get the job done.

The Lord will cut the check once we by faith clear the debt. Clear the debt of fear. Clear the debt of defeatism. Clear the debt of doubt.

When that Divine DEPOSIT hits insufficiency is canceled. Inadequacy is nullified. The Divine DEPOSIT hitting your account neutralizes all of the derogatory activity against your account.

What might seem like the finality of everything is a phenomenal life-taking form. Thru the minuscule adaptations and minute, adoptions conceive transformation that may be unnoticed to the naked eye, nonetheless, undeniably real in the grand scheme of things.

John Borling Major General who served in the United States Air Force survived nearly seven soul-crushing years imprisoned during the Vietnam War in Hanoi Hilton. Creative writing was his therapy. One such poem he penned is entitled **THIS I BELIEVE**

Some are made for mountains, Some prefer the plain,

But each must have self-esteem To bring him home again.

Values come from people,

Assessing their amounts,

Those worthy of respect and pride, All know the striving counts.

Prayer:

Give me the strength to live another day, O God.

Let me not cower in the face of its hardships or fail to fulfill my responsibilities. Let me not lose confidence in others. Despite ingratitude, deceit, or meanness, keep me sweet and pure of heart. Keep me from noticing or providing little stings. Help me to keep my heart pure and to live my life so honestly and courageously that no external failing can dishearten me or take away the delight of conscious honesty.

Open my soul's eyes so that I may see the good in everything as according to Your Word all things work together for good to them who love You and are called according to Your purpose.

Give me a new view of the truth today;

In the name of the great Deliverer, our only Lord, and Savior, Jesus Christ, fill me with the spirit of joy and pleasure, and make me the cup of strength to suffering souls. Amen.

Application: GOOD DAYS BAD DAYS

Divide a sheet of paper by a vertical line. One side title GOOD DAYS. The opposite side caption BAD DAYS. Reflect over two weeks and label the good days and the bad days, respectively. Count it up. Did you have more good days than bad days?

AFFIRMATION:

THE TOUGH TIMES ARE TEMPORARY and the TRIUMPH will be TERRIFIC

GETUPNLIVE:FULLY PERSUADED

> No distrust made him (Abraham) waver concerning the promise of God, but he grew strong in his faith as he gave glory to God, being fully convinced that God was able to do what he had promised.
>
> - Romans 4:20-21NRSV

> I planned my success; I knew it was going to happen.
>
> -Erykah Badu

Sometimes the direction and desire that God puts in your heart seem strange. The distinction and difference are factors to our lack of follow thru and reasons behind our defiance. What God is asking us to do is so dissimilar to our current condition that it tests our obedience to His Sovereign Will. It is imperative that we do what God tells us to. Grateful to connect with others who have the grace to communicate and confirm what God has given you. It becomes increasingly important as one develops and continues his relationship with God that he learns amidst the strange instructions to follow thru. The instruction from the Lord may be unsynoptic, ridiculous, unorthodox, strange, or even weird. The center of God's sovereign will certifies our safety. So, as we obey the instruction, we are drawn closer to the destiny God has in mind. Arriving at destiny is not an all-in-one shot nor will it just fall out of the sky.

Our lives are processional, built in stages, and launched in segments. All these activities co-joined are building you up to who you are to be, where you are to be, and when you are to do it. Mary followed the instructions, and Samson's Nazarite parents followed the instructions.

What is going to draw us to the desired result is when we obey every instruction laid out.

Discerning divine direction and instruction is the first stem and then unwavering dedication must follow.

Don't ask God for an extraordinary opportunity if all you purpose to do is remain average. Many missed opportunities are attributed to lost patience. While soiled and messed up opportunities are due to a lack of patience. The old adage is true: haste makes waste.

The drive is very important. Determination has the power to destroy doubt. If you can't choose you can't CHANGE. Forbid indecision is the impedance to being INCREDIBLE. Our belief must be that we will divinely be directed to the possession of what has been promised to us. That means God has every failure and every feat- every victory.

Faith is so dynamic because it forms dreams and fuels them, too. An even more solemn but accurate reflection is how faithlessness can be fatal. So, Find yourself faith. It helps, no it doesn't just help- it is everything.

It is perplexing how conformity is so interesting, seeing that it is so commonplace. Some are inclined to do so perhaps because compromise many times submits conveyances of power and profit. Yet, conformity has no soul; no ethical obligation.

As we traverse and sojourn it is vitally important that we hold fast to our confidence and our commitment. The good work begun in us will come to full maturation.

Prayer:

God who is merciful and mighty Your power, passion, and promises motivate me to persevere. I thank You for treading the sea and channeling the desert. I am seeking Lord to capture a fresh vision for each day connected to the fixed purpose You've designed for my life. May the people I encounter, the places that I enter, and the predicaments I endure fan the flame of favor to light my path forward. May those flames also consume every impediment, burn away any insecurity along with any measure of defeatism in my mind or forming in my mouth. I am tantalized by the promise of the new creation. Thank you. In Jesus's sublime, sufficient, and spectacular name. Amen.

Application:

Imagine you are being interviewed about your success story. Sit in front of your smartphone and record responses to

1. the Purpose of your work

2. insights that powered your will

3. envision each step from the finish line back to the starting line

AFFIRMATION:

I BELIEVE THAT THE GOOD WORK BEGUN IN ME WILL COME TO FULL BLOOM.

LISTEN UP

"Fools think their own way is right, but the wise listen to advice."

- Proverbs 12:15

Listen or your tongue will keep you deaf

-Ancient Proverb

What comes into our hearing plays out in our lives. And even if filtered, we will not be exempt from some of the playback of spoken words seeping into our perception if not our reality. So then, the right voice matters, because we are so impressionable. Think about how much we honor dead people's wishes and simultaneously refuse to harken to a living person's pleas for help.

Majoring in speaking and minoring in listening is a sure strategy for the abundant production of STUPIDITY.

Hearing and listening are not identical. Hearing refers to the physical process of perceiving sound waves by the ear, while listening implies a conscious effort to pay attention, understand, and interpret the meaning of the sounds. Hearing is a passive activity that happens unconsciously while listening is an active process that requires focus and attention. In short, hearing is the ability to detect sounds, while listening is the ability to make sense of those sounds. Listening produces understanding and meaning. It involves paying attention, processing information, and interpreting the meaning of what is being said in order to respond appropriately or take action. Effective listening can lead to better communication, improved relationships, and increased productivity. It helps to build trust, respect, and empathy between individuals and can prevent misunderstandings and conflicts from arising. When one actively listens to another person, it is beneficial in several ways, including:

1. Feeling heard and understood: When someone takes the time to listen to another's concerns, doubts, or opinions without interrupting or judging, they allow that person to feel seen and heard. This can create a sense of validation and help them feel understood.

2. Developing trust: Being able to communicate in a way that feels safe and secure is important for building trust in any relationship. Active listening can create an environment of trust where people feel comfortable sharing their thoughts and feelings without fear of being judged or criticized.

3. Improving relationships: Listening to others can help develop healthier relationships by improving communication and fostering mutual respect. Effective listening can prevent misunderstandings

and conflicts from arising and promote positive interactions.

4. Identifying needs and offering help: Active listening can help individuals understand the needs of the people they are listening to, which allows them to offer appropriate assistance or support.

By listening to others the exchange is beautified and enhanced as a positive communication environment where people feel understood, validated, and valued is created.

Prestige, prosperity, and power clog our ears. The deafening noise prevents us from hearing a necessary message. Likewise, pride and stubbornness barricade the entrance to wisdom and truth. They will block the door of opportunity and future prospects.

The proof that communication has been received is in the response. When a communication is transmitted a respondent will either engage, ignore, or reject the communication. This will be based on his INTERPRETATION

The truth expressed will wipe out an argument and cancel confusion. It is the withheld and, many times, overlooked truth that issues the continuance of contention. However, the moment truth is undeniably presented which forces everyone to admit the verity of it, the debate is closed. Now, the perpetrator and guilty party may cut a conversation with cynical interjections like "Oh ok" but the truth brings resolve.

Sometimes you gotta wait out and wade in

INTERRUPTIONS ATTENTIVELY; for often, there is a MESSAGE within them, too.

At certain junctures, wisdom says that it is best to let people say their piece, while you savor your victory in peace.

Listening is important to negotiating. In negotiations, it is not just what you want but what the other party wants, as well. So inoculate the other parties who want to leverage your desired end. The best way of doing that is to listen to their needs, vision, and expectations

Prayer:

God who sees my hardships, hears my cries, and helps me when I call; I thank you that you not only look on me but also listen to me. This privilege of praying and communing with You I do not take lightly. Forgive me when I did not actively focus on your direction and the times I ignored Your instruction. Help me Lord, to study to be quiet so that I will be quick to hear and slow to speak. I want to be an impactful listener, I need strength to resist the urge to interrupt. I want to give my family, friends, and anyone providentially placed in my path, the gift of being heard. May the Love of Christ be shown to the world even thru compassionate listening. In the Loving name of Our Lord, AMEN.

Application:

Visit Youtube and play a TED talk. Stop periodically to paraphrase what the speaker discusses and pose a follow-up question.

AFFIRMATION:

I OBSERVE MY INTERNAL RESPONSE, AND ALSO OFFER RESPECT BY CREATING A SAFE SPACE FOR EXPRESSION. I AIM TO ACTIVELY LISTEN FOR OBSCURED MEANINGS.

ELEVATED LIVING

You are saved by God's grace! And God raised us up and seated us in the heavens with Christ Jesus.

- Ephesians 2:5,6 CEB

We are all capable of climbing so much higher than we usually permit ourselves to suppose.

- Octavia Butler

A man was traveling down a rural road late one night when his compact sedan experienced a blowout. Shaken by the sudden mishap, James gathered himself and looked around for a potential rescuer of help. Walking up the winding uphill country road he spots a modest bungalow set back from the road and proceeded cautiously toward the dimly lit front years.

Apprehension arrested James as he strolled closer. James' self-talk began to be as cutting as the crisp night air. He'd determined that whoever opened the door would be irritable with him for the interruption. He hypothesized hostility and not hospitality. James substantiated his assumption by the residence's placement nestled between the trees and distant from street signs, traffic lights, communities, and neighborhoods. With every step away from the street the darker James' image of the person in the dwelling drew. He's an isolationist. He's eccentric. He fully convinced himself the person on the other side of the door was irrational, irate, and emboldened. Such, that when his rapping on the door ceased the latch jingled, the knob turned, and the doorway creaked -James punched the man in the nose and quickly turned from the injured man back to the darkness of the night.

We can skew and sour situations with our subversive suppositions. Opt out of outlooks that are off-base and perfidious. James not only injured someone who was innocent but it leaves him still in need. Living by blind faith even when we cannot physically see or fathom makes us unstoppable in making the trek forward. While being led by fear suffocates and limits us. The toleration of fear onsets the contamination of faith. One sliver of fear unmanaged manifests in wavering. Another evidence of fear manifests in worrying. It is one reason tussling with doubt is a necessary fight. Keeping our objective raised is a constant task. It looks like reflecting on the Divine promises instead of ruminating over problems.

Self-exploration shouldn't be at the cost of someone else's exploitation. Ignoring and being flat-out blind to some things and avoiding toxic interactions will help us to stay free, remain focused and forge on course. Remembering that each person is an instrument of a larger plan is key.

Realigning a network is essential to raising the net worth. Affiliations and associations are important.

Our DNA is fractured and flawed but that space is fixed for Father's intervention. Facing our frailties comes to the forefront as we strive to go up in life. But vulnerability does not have to be a ticking time bomb waiting to blow up our lives into fragments and smithereens. Truly, we must disarm the salaciousness of susceptibility. Drama is an energy drainer, a focus distorter, and a detractor of momentum.

Have a mind to go higher. Nothing negative. You are well able to overcome anything. Any fool can die. It takes imagination to live. We march into victory to the pace of rhythmic patterns that drum our success stroll. Right thinking is critical to arriving in the right spaces and situations. Formulating a brilliant idea is like flipping a light switch that casts bright light into a dim space. The right idea can dismiss dismalness from a situation.

Elevated living is possible when one becomes more conscious of doing than dying. The Psalmist melodizes this in Psalm 49:15 "But God will ransom my soul from the power of the grave for He will receive me."It is possible to acknowledge a situation is bad and have room to BELIEVE circumstances will get better. Cognition does not preclude conviction. Recognizing a hardship doesn't remove the opportunity to rejoice in hope. So, peep the bad news, sure, but elevated living requires that we promote the good news.

Prayer:

Dear God, I come before you today and pray to be propelled into an elevated life. Help me to contour my thoughts, words, and actions always gracefully, lovingly, and with wisdom. All that I would be progressively lifting into a higher state of existence. I practice seeking Your will above all else, for I am certain You know what is best. Carve from within me the courage to take the necessary steps to live the life that you have called me to live. You have taught me to not settle for mediocrity or live in fear, but instead, to soar to new heights. Send, O God, encouragers who help me to grow, learn, and achieve my goals. Also, help me to be a light unto others and inspire them to live an elevated life as well. With You, all things are possible. So, I ask that perseverance comes so that I can overcome the obstacles that I will face, and the assurance that doing all things through Christ who strengthens me is a guarantee. I put on honor on Your name and humbly surrender to Your will full belief that as I humble myself up under Your mighty hand, being exalted is my portion. In Jesus' name, I pray, Amen.

Application:

Write your imaginary eulogy which describes how you'd like to be remembered after you're gone. Completing this exercise reveals how you want to show up in the world so that the necessary shifts that need to occur can be identified. Upon completion of this self-awareness builder, you will be equipped to achieve your higher self better.

AFFIRMATION:

I AM EMPOWERED & EQUIPPED TO ENGINEER THE LIFE I ENVISION.

THE PATH TO YOUR BEST

Possessing inferior or insufficient resources may create an impasse that gridlocks one's grind to achieving their best. But, there are still ways to maximize potential and generate significant progress. Focusing on establishing reliable routines and habits that reinforce positive behaviors and incrementally build desired outcomes is a great strategy. Configuring a consistent schedule for practicing skills, creating the reminder alarm on the smartphone, composing clear and attainable goals with specificity, and keeping track of one's progress to stay motivated is a proven scenario that sets one up for success. Another approach entails seeking out low or no-cost resources, such as online tutorials and certifications, as well as community workshops and mentorship opportunities is another viable strategy, too. Also, networking with community figures and persons in the same niche via social networks can significantly help. With determination, creativity, and deliberate action, even with few resources at one's disposal, championing life and being one's absolute best is possible.

The path to your best is not constricted by the absence of resources but by the lack of imagination. Possessing inferior or insufficient resources may create an impasse that gridlocks one's grind to achieving their best. But, there are still ways to maximize potential and generate significant progress. Focusing on establishing reliable routines and habits that reinforce positive behaviors and incrementally build desired outcomes is a great strategy. Configuring a consistent schedule for practicing skills, creating the reminder alarm on the smartphone, composing clear and attainable goals with specificity, and keeping track of one's progress to stay motivated is a proven scenario that sets one up for success. Another approach entails seeking out low or no-cost resources, such as online tutorials and certifications, as well as community workshops and mentorship opportunities is another viable strategy, too. Also, networking with community figures and persons in the same niche via social networks can significantly help. With determination, creativity, and deliberate action, even with few resources at one's disposal, championing life and being one's absolute best is possible.

Self-reliance can be achieved in many ways besides merely being physically tough.

Our interconnectedness with others should not be neglected or underplayed. Solidarity, in fact, is the missing link between actual systemic change and the formation of flourishing social structures. The harmonious agreement breaks through the shadows of hatred and ruthless savagery. Partnerships and collaborations with a common goal are quite valuable.

Author Stephen Covey suggests that every human has four endowments – self-awareness, conscience, independent will, and creative imagination. These give us the ultimate human freedom… The power to choose, to respond, to change. The path to our best self then can be engineered as we harness choice, changes, and chiming in. We can clear our path that is fogged with fears and clogged with memories by engaging the internal tools of conscientiousness, cognizance, character, and creative imagination.

Prayer:

God who is Alpha and Omega, First and Last,

I yield to the throne of grace because there would be no me without You. In You, I live, breathe, move, and have my being. You know the sections of life where I feel uncertain about my life's direction, and I pray You to guide me to the paths of righteousness for Your namesake. The green pastures, still waters, and even through the valley of the shadows of death, I will travel the course with all those stops as long as I come to dwell in Your house. I believe the path plotted for me will also bring me to the plans prepared for me. Your promises are sure, and I will persevere in possessing all prescribed to me. Holy Spirit activate. Fill me with Your peace as I pursue and press. Grant me that peace that passes all understanding. No matter what problems arrive, I want to stay passionately persuaded concerning Your prerogatives. For producing positive outcomes in my life, I thank you in advance.

I believe the best is yet to come; I only need to remain faithful until death. In the preeminent, powerful, permanent, and precious name of the Prince of Peace, I pray, AMEN.

AFFIRMATION:

I AM CONSCIOUS OF THE CREATION UNDER CONSTRUCTION AND COMPETENT TO COMPLETE IT. MY COMMITMENT OVERSHADOWS ANY CONFLICT.

Application:

Make the investment in an experienced mentor or coach and accelerate the achievement of your goals. A mentor or coach has likely guided scores of people to the success you are setting forth to actualize. Professional executive coaches are skilled in structuring your efforts to maximize effect and keep measurable instruments in place for accountability.

Alternatively, digest all the content of a mentor or coach via their podcasts and published articles along with any other available content. Use the guides and principles consistently.

BE HUMBLE

Humility is the catalyst to your promotion in GOD. The constant reminder of where I came from keeps afresh an appreciation for where I am. Being comfortable being small could very well be the medium that increases your influence. Gideon's army wasn't acceptable until his army was retracted to a smaller force.

Unconditional virtue cannot be expected of any person. All humans carry, at best, a residue of a vice. Every single person walks through life with a shadow of shame tailing him that does not vanish in our most glorious march. The mistakes made in life have an expiration date.

Guarding the purity of one's intention from self-glory and corruption requires constant vigilance. Intentionally incorporating daily acts of selflessness adds a sense of fulfillment and felicity to persons who receive it and to the practitioner, simultaneously. Prioritizing others over one's self shouldn't have permanent primacy, but preferring others and considering others helps harness haughtiness and being puffed up with pride. Simply offering genuine expressions of encouragement, engaging authentically, and actively listening to another's perspective are good examples of selfless moves. Other ways to develop selflessness include holding the door for someone to cross the threshold to an establishment first, volunteering to assist a coworker with a project, or supporting a friend going through a challenging situation. The rewards that come from putting the needs of others above one's own have proven medical benefits, as well as emotional and spiritual blessings. Recurrently engaging in acts of altruism will automatically make a sound effect for those who are recipients and, most assuredly, good byproducts issued to the giver

Being in the public eye means being sighted in the province of hackers and prying eyes. There are bystanders who only want to make inglorious your incredible strides and forward movement.

Self-help doesn't need to turn to self-harm; although it does when we reach the point of self-absorption. Sometimes as we develop and climb the rungs of life's ladder we have a tendency to look down on others with a condescending gaze and a smirk of superiority. However, we should really walk humbly since at any given moment the scales could subvert and the roles could be reversed.

Prayer:

Gracious, Glorious, and Great God, You have promised to raise me up if I humble myself before You. I know today that I cannot achieve on my own and that I need You at all times. It is in You that I live, breathe, and have my being so I humble myself before You, and I beg that You work in and through me today. My time, energy, thoughts, talents, and words are all at Your disposal today. Show me what I don't know and help me improve my understanding of you and your compassion for your people. Use me for your purposes, Lord. I am certain that you will be there for me and raise me up. In Your Strong, Sufficient, and Sovereign Name, I pray, AMEN.

Application:

Be intentional about opening the door for other people whether they are young or old, male or female. Or, offer some other courtesy such as paying it forward in the drive-thru line.

AFFIRMATION:

I AM ABLE TO SEE MYSELF WITH TRUE CLARITY; EYEING THE AREAS TO IMPROVE, IDENTIFYING THE ASPECTS WHICH ARE IMPRESSIVE, AND RESISTING THE URGE TO EMBELLISH WHO I AM.

SHARE YOUR STORY

"I'm delighted to share the signs and miracles that the Most High God has worked in my life."

- Daniel 4:2 CEB

"You got to make your CASE"

-Kanye West

A gift is purposed to be given. This is what makes burying those gifts or neglecting to discover and develop them so brutal and unforgiving. The world needs that very good gift that is deep within. Sharing what we were born to be and conquer. We cannot be everything to everyone and still be true to ourselves. The cemetery is viewed by many as a morbid place, but it is also the most exclusively eclectic treasure trove and exquisite collection of experiences.

Our lives do not commence nor conclude with fairy tale whims. Human existence is littered with illogical, uncertain, and unfair moments. Our human experience is to be retold to light the path for those coming behind us and as a warning to others approaching danger. The ancient Grecian philosopher Plato said "Those who tell stories, rule society"

Let the energy of your story be the drama. Sharing your story helps you to become forever linked to your loved ones and acquaintances in the way folksinger Peggy Seeger would lyricize about her friend when she sang

"He died, but he is still in my present tense."

When we tell our stories, we also invoke the names of others, sometimes who have passed on from this physical terrain but yet are still impacting and influencing our lives. I often speak of the wisdom of Mrs. Sarah Virginia

Cady Bulger, my maternal grandmother. I share conversation snippets I've shared with my paternal grandfather Mr. Samuel Shine Sr that are so vivid listener and have said to me: I want to meet him. I have to disappoint them by letting them know they have passed on.

People are often seen for what they do and meanwhile who they are is entirely missed, misrepresented, or misunderstood. Don't waste away shying from telling your story, tell someone. What if your next blessing was hinged on sharing your story? Nothing precludes one from telling a story and being the story told. Each of us has a story and our detailed accounts can change the lives of others around us when we divulge them.

Prayer:

Holy and Righteous God, I am grateful that You created me and carved me out of someone else's story to uniquely have my own story that I can share with others. I pray that you give me the courage and confidence to speak openly about the experiences that have shaped me into the person I am today. I want the telling of my story to be seasoned words to someone in a weary season. I ask You, Lord, to help me catalyze change among others as we connect to similar struggles and successes common in our stories. May my testimony bring hope, healing, and help to those who need it most. Please guide my words and actions as I share my journey. May everything I say and do be a reflection of your love and compassion.

Thank you, God, for the precious gift of life and the moments that have brought me to where I am today. May my story bring glory to your name as I courageously share it. In Jesus' name, I pray. Amen.

AFFIRMATION:

MY INDIVIDUAL JOURNEY IS VALUABLE AND SHO WING MY UNIQUE PERSPECTIVE MATTERS.

Application:

Reflect on a newsworthy scene from the day. Inquire of yourself: "If I had to tell a story from today, what would it be?" It doesn't have to be a sentinel moment, just a significant one that stuck out. It could be an interaction that warmed your heart, an epiphany, or even a humorous encounter. Write down the date and a one-paragraph summary of that moment.

MARK THE MOMENT

> "You don't really know about tomorrow. What is your life like? You are a mist that appears for only a short while before it vanishes."
>
> -James 4:14 CEB

> "All we have to decide is what to do with the time that is given us."
>
> -J.R.R. Tolkien

A lesson can be taken from the cuckoo clock. As each hour strikes it still sings...it bursts thru the doors and makes its presence an unforgettable moment with regularly scheduled encore performances

Living in the moment is noticing death slouching toward me from the corner of the room and being so focused on possibilities that I pay it not much mind. With each passing day, it is more and more apparent that an ability to accomplish anything is attached to the advantage my abilities aid in the struggle.

Being intentional about honoring every moment will most times result in a positive outcome. Every closure isn't because of failure. A shift can very much look like a fracture. We honor the moment by being purposeful, productive, and positive. Service to purpose should be elevated over being stuck on a personality. The greater good of an organization may, at a point, beckon for transitions to take place in one position or another of the group, firm, company, or social entity. We honor moments well by moving with a constructive outlook. A positive perspective in any moment is a way to honor it. The Apostle Paul does this on several occasions. In his letter to the Romans, he says "We know that God works all things together for good for the ones who love God, for those who are called according to his purpose."(Romans 8:28 CEB). While imprisoned he sends a letter of encouragement to the church at Philippi saying whether abased or abounding he has learned to be content. Not only do we appreciate moments thru being purposeful and positive, but also in being productive. Making it happen no matter what time it is or what encumbrances may be along the path, proves how much one cherishes the privilege of more time. Honoring a moment produces joy in the person and from the predicament.

Welcome the new day's arrival with expectancy, exuberance, and a strong embrace. Lie down every evening with a brimming heart of gratitude. Every day is inestimably valuable. As such, the time afforded to us should be stewarded well and enjoyed. Like an exotic coffee or full-bodied wine, time should be sipped and savored. Because hoarding time presumptuously may be for an hour that never arrives.

 Life's most important moments are the ones that make you realize there is no turning back. Having crossed the line, you are permanently on the other side. Like it or not, everything changes at this moment. Holding on to the present to prevent the oncoming challenges is futile.

Prayer:

Lord I thank You for the higher power You've supplied to me, and Your holy presence that surrounds me. I need you to help me make good use of the time I have and am in. Equip me to be able to redeem the time. I acknowledge the significance and importance of this moment, and I ask You God to help me like the sons of Issachar to discern the times so that I can develop beyond the time. Long after my physical presence has disappeared I want my works to still speak for me and glorify You. May Your divine presence move me forward with purpose, because I know I need to stand with clarity of mind and with courageous motivation. I realize that I can only best do that with you accompanying me. As I come before you today, I ask for your guidance and presence to mark this moment in my life. Open my eyes to see the opportunities that present themselves and orient me to embrace the changes that come my way. In this moment, I place my trust in Your guidance and wisdom. May your love surround me and guide me every step of the way. Amen.

Application:

It's the little things...a smile, a photo, a seashell, a handkerchief, a fragrance bottle, or a broach. There are many collectible items that we accumulate over a lifetime linked to a bit of nostalgia. These small treasures are invaluable because they evoke cherished memories of times gone by. So, start a memory box. A memory box is a loving place to store the little mementos that you alone or possibly with a loved one cherished. Personalize it with your unique design on it. Then, create a storage space for easy retrieval, so that you and your loved ones can mark your special moments and reminisce about those lovely days.

AFFIRMATION:

I HAVE A RELEVANT PLACE AND HOLD A RICH
PURPOSE TO REACH HELPFUL PROGRESS

CELEBRATE SMALL WINS

Always be joyful. Never stop praying. Whatever happens, give thanks, because it is God's will in Christ Jesus that you do this.

~ I Thessalonians 5:16-18 GWT

"Celebrating the small wins is a great way to build confidence and start feeling better about yourself."

— Abhishek Ratna

I've come to discover the satiety produced by success and goal attainment isn't savored most at the achievement of goals, but from struggling vigorously. It has been the dips, the debits, and deconstruction that is responsible in part for the laurels worn today. So, celebrating each milestone along the way becomes incredibly important. The cumulative effect of seemingly inconsequential daily changes and breakthroughs can have a stunning impact once enough time has elapsed.

Standing atop where others are trying to reach doesn't shirk back or diminish the journey. Truth is, some antagonizing characters or conditions are a badge of honor that should proudly adorn us as they are proofs of resiliency and resourcefulness. The desire for abundance is a choice. The ability to manage it is the result of discipline. Defeatism is not your native language, and neither is unbelief.

Major amelioration can be produced from minor achievements. While everything is not finished, something has been fixed and founded. What fuels participation in the project's completion is to passionately celebrate that progress.

A finite, finished, and fully executed outcome of moderate importance is considered a little win. A single, seemingly insignificant victory might not seem worth celebrating alone. However, a pattern's visibility becomes visible that may recruit supporters, remove saboteurs, and reduce resistance to following ideas if established through a sequence of victories at minuscule but meaningful tasks. Small victories are opportunities that are organizable, and they yield observable results.

The odd thing about winning is that it will arouse some people to cheer and others to chide. Just remember the bigger the TRIAL; the bigger the TROPHY. Settling can become a SEDATIVE. LET EVERY ADVERSE FORCE CONVERGE. Decline the invitation to join the confederacy of quitters. Don't forget, super-sized aspirations aren't the only ingredients to success. Small achievements are too.

Prayer:

Mountain moving, Majestic, and my Marvelous Maker, You stepped into nothingness, spinning, sewing, and swirling nothing together until they became something remarkable.

Then, You turned the light on so that what you did in the darkness and bleakness would be well-known. God, You specialize in superbness from smallness. You supplanted redemption in the womb of a virgin. Elijah heard the abundance of rain while looking at a cloud the size of a man's fist. The Son of God even fed a multitude with a little one's lunch.

Help me hold to my hope that great things come from small things. I implore You're assisting me in identifying my strengths and my gifts. I want You to be pleased with my use of them, not self-servicing only, but in ways beneficial to those around me, too. I want to be a blessing to all who I come in contact with. I pray that I always remember to give you the glory and honor for all I achieve, knowing that it is only through your might that I make anything praiseworthy in this world. In Jesus' name, I pray, Amen.

Application:

It is said that "success leaves clues". Find a success story to study. After becoming familiar with the account:

1. Identify the small wins in the journey to the big win.

2. Connect the wins to the pivots.

3. Compose inspiring statements that will incentivize you toward achievement

AFFIRMATION:

MY BUDDING BELIEF IS INDEED BONAFIDE FAITH. I AM JUST AS ELATED OVER THE INCREMENTAL BLESSINGS OF THE LORD AS WITH THE OVERSIZED ONES.

AS AN ACT OF WORSHIP

"If you want to set your heart right, then pray to him. If you're holding on to sin, put it far away, and don't let injustice live in your tent.

- Job 11:13,14 GWT

"From God to us to others."

- Ray Pritchard

God is with us, around us, and in us-even despite us. We are created beings who belong in the Creator's presence. Any other reality is diluted, distorted, and dreadfully dissatisfying. It is impossible to be the best version of ourselves outside God's presence. By being genuine, gracious, and giving we attract God's presence, simultaneously bringing God pleasure. For, these are acts of praise which the Lord lives in.

To worship is to be stirred to a spiritual existence through contact with God's holiness that fills the mind with God's truth, cleanses the imagination thru God's beneficence, welcomes God's love into one's heart, and commits one's will to the Divine plan. We can only worship God to the level of our awareness of His revelation. Receptiveness and reverence heighten our attentiveness to God's appearance.

The Sovereign governance of God is obligatory to our worship. The fact that God is in control invites us to worship God. The sufficient grace of God gives us the pattern and grants us permission to worship!

Worship can take various forms depending on cultural, religious, and personal preferences. One form of worship is congregational singing, where a group sings hymns or sacred songs expressing their faith and devotion to a higher power. Another form is prayer, which people passionately present individually or collectively and may involve being prostrate, kneeling, clasping hands, or other bodily gestures. Worship can also include meditation, where an individual or group focuses on thoughts or feelings, usually related to spiritual or philosophical themes. Some people may also engage in fasting, where they abstain from food or other activities to show reverence and devotion to a Power greater than themselves. Other forms of worship include dance, chanting, reading religious texts aloud, and participating in sacraments or rituals. Ultimately, choosing the form of expressing adulation is a personal decision and may evolve as individuals seek to deepen their spiritual connection.

Prayer:

All Sapient & Sovereign God, You are the Creator and Sustainer of everything that exists, and I'm grateful for your loving kindness and faithfulness. I praise your holy name and acknowledge your sovereignty over all things. Your mighty power and infinite wisdom tremendously humble me. Coming before your presence, I echo the exclamation of Isaiah and its similar intensity "Woe is me, for I am undone." Your light makes visible my limitations. I need you, Lord, to build me up where I am torn down and strengthen me where I am weak. Wash me anew so that I am clean.

Help me to live an honorable life that empowers me to do Your will. Grant me wisdom, understanding, and discernment to navigate life's challenges and serve others with humility and compassion. I surrender my worries, fears, and doubts to you and trust in your unfailing love and grace. May your Holy Spirit guide me, inspire me, and transform me. I pray for your people's and the world's needs that your mercy and justice may reign and your kingdom come on earth as in heaven. Thank you for hearing my prayer and for your never-ending presence. In Jesus' name, I pray. Amen.

AFFIRMATION:

I CHASE DOWN GOD'S PRESENCE. I CHOOSE TO DECLARE THE LORD IS WORTHY AND CHERISH DOING THE SOVEREIGN WILL.

Application:

Worship walking is a practice of putting feet to our prayers as one goes about to different places in the city or neighborhood. An alternative activity is to find and hold photos of different landmarks while praying for a few minutes over them.

MAKE YOUR OWN MARK

"Let your light so shine before men, that they may see your good works and glorify your Father in heaven.

- Matthew 5:16 NKJV

"Make your mark in the world with divine ink: love."

— Matshona Dhliwayo

My ways of being are the alchemy of my personality, not defects. It is a substance from my spirit that colors the world, seasons the taste of an experience, and adds texture to what is expressed.

It becomes important to not allow desperation to distract, detour, or become a diversion. With intentionality, I have to move in a deliberate step, determinedly.

The war is waged and some of us still do not know what our weapon looks like or how they've been wielded. Wealthy, winning warriors have tapped into working the weapon...Weary warriors have grown frustrated with a tool they cannot figure out.

The influence of individuals has a pivotal role to play in the numerous ways in shaping organizations and engineering impactful interactions. Leadership is an example of one of these things. Charismatic and knowledgeable persons energize, motivate, and inspire their team to be productive, innovative, and efficient. The synergism sparked from that provides the team members with a clear vision, support, and encouragement while encouraging them to take measured risks. The approach that a leader takes can also affect the culture of the organization as well as how the members of the team interact with one another.

Communication abilities are an additional illustration of the individual influence that can affect companies.

Communicating with clarity can strengthen interpersonal bonds and boost collaboration, contributing to increased productivity. In addition to this, it can prevent misunderstandings, breakdowns in communication, and disputes from occurring. On the other hand, inadequate communication skills restrict one's ability to exert influence, lead to confusion, and demotivate team members. Therefore, developing one's communication abilities can assist individuals in making constructive contributions to organizations.

Making our own mark in the world includes using our voice, and value and employing every other virtue to make something irreversible, indelible, and indestructible. We can make our own mark in how we make others feel.

Making your mark in a world filled with so many preexisting markings and indentations does require intrapersonal skills, introspection, and reflection on one's beliefs, values, and goals. Refining resiliency in rough situations and rifts and an agile survival instinct highlight our journeys and personal evolutions, which are translatable for meaningful manifests to guide others.

Prayer:

Heavenly Father, I believe that who I am is enough since You created me, beautifully and wonderfully. My malfunction is in the sin I commit and when I fall short of Your will. I seek your forgiveness and correction in order that I will return to who You've designed me to be. Thank you for purposely providing a place and space for me to advance Your Sovereign plan. May my work, words, witness, and worship influence and engage those around me to the Glory of the Father. I pray earnestly to be God's vessel, AMEN.

Application:

Find a community volunteer opportunity and sign-up. Or, identify a worthy cause to team up with. This will also sponsor a networking opportunity. Meet new people, learn new skills, or even sharpen old ones.

AFFIRMATION:

I ENCOURAGE, INSPIRE & ILLUMINATE. SO, I DON'T PRODUCE EMPTY INTERACTIONS

EQUIPPED WITH GOD'S WORD

" Whoever gives thought to the word will discover good, and blessed is he who trusts in the LORD."

- Proverbs 16:20 ESV

"The Bible is not a Christian owner's manual but a story — a diverse story of God and how his people have connected with him over the centuries, in changing circumstances and situations."

~Peter Enns

Wisdom is in weighing the worth of what people say. The Word of God is a wealth of prognostic AFFIRMATIONs to make us more wholesome. God's Word is the most valuable instrument that ensures spiritual survival and increases personal growth. Paul helps Timothy recall his unique experience of how the Holy Scriptures made even him wise enough to foster faith in Christ Jesus to obtain salvation.

A substantial detriment to making personal benchmarks is ignorance of God's Word. The legitimacy of ancient Scripture surfaces in the age of the written Holy texts, and the number of persons whose teachings have transformatively been impactful to them validate it as trustworthy content. Moreover, the innumerable references back to the Scriptures or its characters are evincive of its reliability. The Scriptures retell to us from a different vantage history, teaching its readers wisdom, and are pouring with idioms that thoroughly explain the cycle of life.

Scripture holds immense value for various communities of faith worldwide. The collection of sacred texts and stories provides millions of people with guidance, wisdom, and inspiration. The Bible and other religious texts also contain lessons that help seekers, skeptics, and believers navigate their lives and uphold the principles of their faith. Scripture can offer a sense of hope, comfort, and assurance during difficult times, in addition to supplying instructions on how to lead a virtuous and fulfilling life. The value of scripture lies in its ability to enhance one's spiritual life and promote social justice, communal harmony, and interfaith understanding.

In addition to its spiritual benefits, the inspired Word of God can also have practical value. The moral teachings and ethical principles found in many religious texts can guide day-to-day decision-making at both personal and societal levels. For instance, the Bible's " Golden Rule," which instructs individuals to "treat others as they would like to be treated, " is a foundation for ethical behavior in many cultures and predates the written scrolls. Furthermore, what we glean from religious teachings incites kindness, courtesy, and compassion in persons towards others, which can lead to a greater sense of empathy, care, and altruism. Overall, the value of scripture extends beyond the individual and has the potential to promote healthy, balanced, and peaceful societies. As people apply the Scriptures there is no denying its effectiveness against evil powers, ideals, and projections.

PRAYER:

Dear Lord, The sacred words of Scripture that I am holding and reading fill me with awe because of the knowledge and the truth that they carry. When examining the scriptures, I discover answers to questions and develop questions to ask. Please assist me in approaching these words with the appropriate amount of humility, open-mindedness, and a desire to learn. Please give me the understanding, clarity, and discernment I need to comprehend the messages you are attempting to convey through these inspired passages. I want with fresh eyes to hear what You are communicating to me. So, I come before You in the hope that You will direct my path and be present with me while I study the Bible to apply its relevant teachings to my life better.

Show me how to look beyond the words and pages so that I might hear Your voice in the stories, verses, and parables that the Bible contains. I pray that the people whose lives I study to find models of faith and tenacity to guide my own will be a source of motivation for me.

May I apply Scripture to my spiritual development and the spiritual maturing of others close to me? To those with the greatest need for it, may it be a source of consolation, direction, and hope. Your will, for me, is to put its lessons into practice in my day-to-day life in a way that is not only compassionate but also just and comprehensive.

I ask that You enlighten me so that I can better comprehend and use the wisdom attained through these holy writings that strengthen my connection to You and better serve others in Your name. Amen.

AFFIRMATION:

I AM EQUIPPED WITH THE WORD OF GOD TO FULFILL MY LIFE'S CALL WITH CONFIDENCE, CLARITY, AND COMPASSION.

Application:

Rewrite the Verse - Take a favorite verse and rewrite it with today's vernacular and popular words or use an emoji.

GOD HAS YOU COVERED

In peace I will both lie down and sleep; for you alone, O Lord, make me dwell in safety.

- Psalm 4:8

The safest place in all the world is in the will of God, and the safest protection in all the world is the name of God.

~ Warren Wiersbe

God has got you covered. By solidifying the certainty of that statement, serenity we receive. So, what is spectacular is that I can have peace in God while simultaneously surrounded by a problem. Amid stormy circumstances, like Peter, we too can make supernatural steps in the presence of our Savior. The added blessing is should our sights be summoned to the startling effects around us, and we begin to slip into the sea, He will save us.

Have you ever been stuck in a fight that, perceivably, was the hardest of your life? Perhaps even it is your present predicament. Be encouraged that your situation is impermanent, with God being intentional, immutable, imperishable, and incontestable. The Lord will put up walls to secure you and doors to keep you safe.

As a child I remember being taught the song: He's got the whole world, in His hands. You and me brother, You and me sister in His hands. God in Divine strength has us covered. Even when malicious motivations are in motion against us, the Almighty One will maneuver you around every demonic plan coming into your life. Active shooters will alarm us. Yes! The threat of weaponized racism does create agony. The array of other antagonizing situations does annoy and anger us. But don't fall prey to an affiliation with what is against you that you miss who is for you. You are not without an assistant. You are not left without an advocate. You still have an ally in the Almighty.

God is fighting against what is frightening you. It is important to believe that when we cannot avert danger, God is present with us. The Lord is there and reveals God's divine self in the half-lit places. God does not abandon us but makes God's self a refuge when we are in hard places. God is there when to rekindle when we are in hopeless places.

Remember that Divine protection from on High presents itself in warnings and even interventions involving other individuals employed by God to extend to us comfort, support, and tangible assistance when needed. We are never alone even when we are in the bleakest of settings. The embrace of unconditional love shields us from the worst even when are all too aware that we aren't at our best.

We may hear the terror, we may see the trouble but we will enjoy the triumph from the name of the Lord being a strong tower.

Prayer:

Yahweh El-Roi, You are the God who sees me. You alone are worthy of admiration for sustaining and stabilizing me. I am praying along with all Your other children. God, you have an outpour of grace which becomes an overflow of greatness. My attempts to do right often require divine guidance, and my earnestness in diligently responding wanes. I ask that You be my shield and buckler. Make an impasse so that hurt, harm, danger, nor alarm can overtake me. May your precious blood cover me and keep me safe. I know that my Redeemer lives. So, I am not fearful when weapons form against me because I know they are without functionality with You surrounding me. Thank You for faithful watch over me to save me from me, even. You are constantly aware of my going out along with my coming in. Keep me in your care, I pray. AMEN.

AFFIRMATION:

I AM COVERED UNDER GOD'S WINGS, AND KEPT FOR GOD'S WATCH

Application:

Compile a list of the important things in your life. Then, pray and give them into the Lord's faithful hands. Ask God to come alongside your faith needed to trust completely the Divine Will.

STRETCH BEFORE YOU START

" Show yourself in all respects to be a model of good works, and in your teaching show integrity, dignity, *Titus 2:7 ESV*

What would life be if we had no courage to attempt anything?"

– Vincent Van Gogh

Humanity was Divinely crafted to transcend ordinary possibilities. One's achievements can reach any height desired. As a result, stretching oneself to excel has paramount significance. Stretching in physicality, spirituality, and mentality are equally important.

Before initiating a new adventure or even a new day stretch your spirituality. Karl Barth said once, "To clasp the hands in prayer is the beginning of an uprising against the disorder of the world" An intangible practice can make incredible

The tension created by our various occupying roles, whether at home, in our jobs, or even in social settings, is taxing on the self. The physical, emotional, and mental exertion required to function is intense on multiple levels. It is not difficult to fathom how easily even outstanding leaders might struggle to keep a balance in their lives.

Extending the body's physicality and breaking a sedentary posture has surpassing benefits beyond increasing flexibility or enhancing the effectiveness of movements. There is a proven correlation between low intensity stretching to a pleasant mood and the improved mood status of those who consistently practice physical stretching. Physiological factors, such as reduced cortisol levels, improved attention and balance, and heightened activity in the neurological and neural systems, all contribute, in their unique ways, to an enhanced overall quality of life.

Cognitive stretching is an integral part of learning that involves increasing mental flexibility.

A millennium of institutionalized learning has demonstrated that there is simply no end to studying any specific subject. The context of this information and digital age, where the globe has shrunk to the distance of a few keystrokes, plunges us into the open world. Our minds are forcibly, continuously stretched, and perpetually exposed to this environment.

Cognitive stretching curtails perfectionism. Also, an extension of the mind creates pleasure. It can be fun.

The gap between full and partial knowledge keeps us engaged in the quest for learning. Mental flexibility helps us circumvent behaviors that create ruts, strengthening one's ability to switch between thinking about two different concepts and thinking about multiple ideas simultaneously. Stretching the mind is stressful, stimulating, and satisfying. These are necessary sensory outcomes for our work, the family we are in a relationship with, and the community with which we are intertwined. Carve out a tiny sliver of time to yourself and stretch before diving headfirst into the chaos of your day. Both your body and your mind will be grateful that you did this. From this, you may produce feelings that result in increased vitality, productivity, and concentration.

Prayer:

Author of the Inception and Architect of the end, You, who was, and is, and shall come. I'm at the threshold of a new beginning. I have an unshakable conviction that since You created me, God, you will keep me. Before I go, Before I gain, Before I get to the goal - I seek Your presence to be active with me. I share the Psalter's longing as the deer panteth thirsty for the water brook, so too does my soul, long after the Living God. I understand that my way will not always be easy. Strengthen me, I pray, where I am weak, stabilize me where I am vulnerable, and situate me where I will be most valuable. Grace me, please, with a finisher's anointing. You have begun a good work in me, for me, and in spite of me that will materialize, and I thank you. In the Redeeming, Reigning, and Returning Name of Our Lord, Jesus Christ, AMEN.

AFFIRMATION:

I AM CREATED TO GO SOMEWHERE. I AM CONFIGURED TO GO SUCCEED. I CONCENTRATE & SEIZE THE GOAL.

Application:

Before beginning your main task, take 10-15 minutes to engage in a creative outlet where the free expression of your feelings is possible. Examples:

1. Pick up an instrument and just freestyle notes

2. Pick up a coloring book and color

3. Write out one goal or dream multiple times

WITH THE TRUTH

" Jesus said to the Jews who believed in him, "You are truly my disciples if you remain faithful to my teaching. Then you will know the truth, and the truth will set you free."

John 8:31,32 CEB

He that takes truth for his guide, and duty for his end, may safely trust God's providence to lead him alright.

-Blaise Pascal

The human mind incessantly searches for the origin and object of things. The space we dwell in must be explored, searched, and studied —with an outcome bearing more substantial meaning for our existence. Philosophers, Scientists, and Anthropologists begin with the investigative inquiry of what, who, where, and when to address the why ultimately.

I had rather believe all the fables in the Legend, the Talmud, and Alcoram than assume this universe frame is without mind. Therefore, God never wrought miracles to convince atheism because God's ordinary works convince it.

The origin and object of the world are revealed in the persona of God's Son. You see, truth is not a collection of facts, but THE Truth is Jesus Christ Himself. He declares himself to be such when he asserts his Messiahship with the disciples in the claim, "I am the Way, THE TRUTH, and the LIFE."

Truth is a powerful force capable of transforming our lives, relationships, and the world around us. Truth allows us to confront our fears, biases, and limitations and to grow and expand beyond them. It enables us to make informed decisions, build deeper connections with others, and positively contribute to society. Whether discovering the truth about ourselves, others, or our world, the pursuit of truth is imperative to living an authentic, fulfilling, and meaningful life.

While discovering the truth can be challenging, it is also a journey that is rife with rewards. It invites us to engage in the beauty of life, learn and grow through experiences, and make a positive impact in the world. We can cultivate a sense of inner peace and freedom when we strive for truth, even when it is uncomfortable or difficult. Ultimately, when centered in truth, we live more authentically, love at a greater depth, and become poised to latch onto our highest potential.

Despite the value of truth, many people fall into the trap of disconnecting from it. There are numerous reasons why people might do so, including fear, discomfort, and self-protection. Sometimes, discovering the truth can challenge our deeply ingrained beliefs or force us to face uncomfortable realities that we would rather avoid.

Additionally, societal pressures or groupthink may cause individuals to disconnect from the truth to maintain a sense of acceptance or belonging.

Other factors like confirmation bias, misinformation, and disinformation can also contribute to a disconnect from truth. When an unconscious bias or belief is reinforced by information, we tend to accept it as actual and accurate, even if it is not based on evidence. Misinformation, or the spread of wrong messages, can further confuse and mislead those seeking the truth. Disinformation, or the deliberate spread of false information, can be used to manipulate or gain control over individuals or groups.

Those who disconnect from the truth do so for many diverging reasons, some of which may be subconscious or external influences. However, it is essential to recognize the value of truth and seek it out to live an authentic and fulfilling life. The truth assigns inconvertible value to one's purpose. The truth is never trifling and will always, by its very nature, confront trickery, flattery, and treachery.

When a person lies, he gives in to his own frailty. Sometimes we are guilty of lying to ourselves.

Unfortunately, trust is quite fragile. When there is trust between partners, anything is possible. The exceptional can emerge from any kind of partnership, be it a professional alliance, a romantic partnership, or a treaty between states. The most hurtful of all betrayals is one that causes trust to be broken or fail. The true cost of treachery is lost on those who do not respect loyalty and honesty. I would rather be hurt now because you left than die because you lingered. Keeping people too long can lead to their deviant mindset fermenting into destructive concoctions that corrode and corrupt the work environment, and what is stored up, desecrate an organization, and even tarnish the best personal qualities one might possess.

The only thing worse than a lie is a lie that gets multiplied and exponentiated. In a world where untruths are proffered to puppeteer unsuspecting people groups; be prepared to be dismissed if deceit is prohibited. The rhythm of a person's behavior patterns and cycles reveals the truth more than words. There is no pocket of darkness that the light of God won't find, and God calls God's self-truth.

Prayer:

Blessed are You, Yahweh, Revealer of Truth, who holds me up by Your Mighty power and heals me with Your Merciful presence. Thank you God, for hearing the voice of my heart with maternal instinct. Amplify the soft calm voice so that I may receive your truth wholeheartedly. Reveal the truth to me and help me, Lord, to radiate authenticity thru every part of my life so that there is no room for false notions or false narratives. I follow You as the Way, the Life, and the Truth. In Jesus, Name. AMEN...

AFFIRMATION:

I ATTUNE MY LISTENING ABILITIES TO HEAR ONLY THE TRUTH SO THAT I SPEAK THE TRUTH TO MYSELF. I TURN MY BACK ON LIES.

Application:

Confession is good for the soul. Write a confessional. Read it back and then destroy it by ripping it or shredding it. Doing this is an act of coming to terms with the truth about a circumstance or situation.

TAKE ANOTHER LOOK

" Then Elisha prayed and said, "O Lord, please open his eyes that he may see." So the Lord opened the eyes of the young man, and he saw, and behold, the mountain was full of horses and chariots of fire all around Elisha.

- II Kings 6:17 ESV

"Look at everything as though you are seeing it either for the first

or last time, then your time on earth will be filled with glory."

— Betty Smith

I mind my own business, yet I am aware and attentive. When we have self-awareness along with situational awareness, and strong interpersonal skills, we can with agility explore a social landscape.

It is not only important to have a fresh perspective, but it is imperative to identify relevant points of reference as well. An old map is useless in discovering, navigating, or exploring a new land. Personally, I have been frustrated more times than once when traveling the interstate and the GPS hasn't updated and I miss an exit as a result.

Many benefits populate from clarifying perspective, including adept problem-solving, amplified communication, and authentic empathy. First, re-aligning perspective can help individuals to approach problems or challenges from a fresh and more objective viewpoint.

Being a quick-on-the-feet solutionist can lead to identifying new or innovative answers they might not have considered otherwise, leading to more effective decision-making. A renewed perspective can also improve communication skills by enabling individuals to articulate their points of view and ideas concisely while being receptive to the vantages of others. Better collaboration, understanding, and fewer misunderstandings happen. A third resulting advantage to clarified perspective is increased empathy which helps people to understand and appreciate the experiences, thoughts, and feelings of others. It can help individuals see issues from different angles and establish better connections with those around them. Understanding different perspectives can foster a more inclusive and respectful environment where people with different backgrounds, beliefs, or experiences feel valued and respected.

An advantageous act for the self and society is to build make-shift observatories from which to see life and the world, differently. A seat outside a local coffee shop, perhaps, noticing the pedestrians marching the crosswalk. Or, a dusk park bench might be the spot to perch the wooden slant and peep at nature in a wondrous display. A revolutionary perspective might even be reached by sliding steps aback, breathing in as deeply as the darkness which swallows the interior of a well and dashes a gaze on something previously unseen.

Prayer:

Dear God, I am praying for the divine revolutionizing of my outlook and perspective. I need fresh reimagination to overpower the redundancy that compasses me. I need another take. Perhaps another turn. Remind me that in every limitation, there is a lesson. You turn chaos to calm. You bring blessings out of bleakness. Forgive me for not seeing with spiritual sight. Sensitize my eyes that I would hear and perceive spiritually, and sanitize my ears that I would see keenly. Sanctify my heart Lord so that I can with compelling clarity value change and view transformation. Guide me to navigate my negative outlook and see the good in everything around me. I desire to approach each day with a positive attitude, open-mindedness, and compassion for those around me. Remind me that every challenge I face is an opportunity to grow, and every obstacle is an opportunity for me to learn. Help me to focus on the blessings in my life and to appreciate the simple things that bring me joy. Thank you for your unwavering love and guidance. Amen.

AFFIRMATION:

I CHOOSE TO SEE GOOD AND CHERISH THE GIFT OF LIFE.

Application:

Compare and Contrast a breaking news story. Identify the bias or slant from the source you read or listened to.

Made in the USA
Columbia, SC
29 August 2024

41295545R00120